The VC leader crouched next to Vo and gently lifted his head

"You see the power of the People's Army? You see what we can do?"

Vo nodded slowly. His lips and mouth were dry, so it was hard for him to speak. He wanted water, but was afraid to ask, in case he angered the Vietcong officer.

"The Americans and the puppet soldiers did nothing to help you here tonight. They throw you away like garbage. They flee to the cities to lie with whores. They corrupt and taint, then try to fix it with their worthless paper money. They care nothing for the Vietnamese people."

The VC officer was right. Vo *had* seen the Americans flee the hamlet, closely followed by the ARVN. Again Vo nodded.

"Then you know why I do what I must. It is because you have embraced the Americans and their puppets." The officer laid Vo's head on the ground, drew his pistol and fired point-blank at the villager.

"A lesson for everyone."

Also available by Eric Helm:

VIETNAM: GROUND ZERO ™

HAMLET

ERIC HELM

A GOLD EAGLE BOOK FROM
WORLDWIDE ®

TORONTO · NEW YORK · LONDON · PARIS
AMSTERDAM · STOCKHOLM · HAMBURG
ATHENS · MILAN · TOKYO · SYDNEY

First edition October 1988

ISBN 0-373-62714-9

VIETNAM: GROUND ZERO™
HAMLET

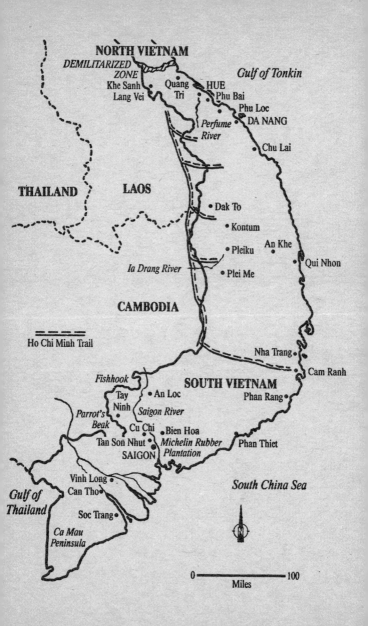

PROLOGUE

THE HAMLET OF DUC
BANG, WAR ZONE C
REPUBLIC OF VIETNAM

The Americans had gone, taking the ARVN personnel with them. The pressures of Tet and the assaults on the district, province and national capital had caused officials to reevaluate the importance of every military installation. The Americans had left a few weapons behind so that the villagers wouldn't be completely defenseless, but these were a collection of bolt-action and semiautomatic rifles that had been obsolete even during Korea. There were no machine guns or mortars and only a few hand grenades. The command in Saigon had convinced themselves that such weapons were more than the villagers required and they would all be safe while the Americans fought the real war elsewhere in South Vietnam.

That had not been the case.

The Vietcong, knowing that the target was ripe, hit the hamlet just after midnight, on the same day the Americans left. It began with a mortar and rocket attack that reduced the main defensive structures to smoking ruins in a matter of minutes. The concrete-reinforced bunker that had housed the Browning M-2 .50-caliber machine gun and the two M-60s was destroyed by a satchel charge because the Vietcong didn't know those weapons had been removed. The explosion threw chunks of cement over the whole village, leaving little more than a crater after the charge detonated.

The bunkers on both sides of it, constructed of sandbags and thick logs, were targeted by the VC mortar crews. The bunkers were saturated with incoming rounds that slowly tore them apart. Had there been any defenders in them, the men would have died quickly, their bodies ripped to shreds by the red-hot shrapnel.

The villagers hid in the center of the hamlet near the newly constructed concrete arms locker, watching the destruction of the defensive ring that had been the pride of the American soldiers. The fifteen men who had formed the core of the defense force hid with the rest of the people, waiting for the Vietcong to come for them. A few villagers clutched the weapons that had been left, but none of them ventured into the rain of destruction.

From outside the hamlet, somewhere on the other side of the rice paddies in the tree line, came the rising note from a bugle. Whistles filled the night and a machine gun started firing, its bullets ripping through the darkness. Tracers flashed overhead.

Two of the defenders, pushed into action by angry looks from their friends, ran from the protection of the arms locker. They kept low, like people struggling against the force of a storm.

The first man reached a corner bunker that hadn't been hit. He crouched behind it and aimed his rifle. In the dark, he could barely discern any images: a smudge in the distance that was the tree line, and the shimmering silver surface of the water in the rice paddies. The hammering of the machine gun drifted to him on a light breeze, sounding like a string of Tet firecrackers snapping in the next village. The muzzle-flashes were a distant flickering that looked festive rather than deadly.

Following the instructions he'd been given by the Americans over the weeks they had been there teaching, he worked the bolt of his rifle, chambering a round. He flicked off the safety and sighted over the top of his weapon, not using the sights. He saw nothing that could be a target and held his fire.

To his right, the second man threw himself to the ground and then dropped his weapon. He covered his head with his hands and squeezed his eyes shut, not wanting to see. His ragged breathing stirred up tiny puffs of dust. The ground was only an inch from his lips. He could taste the dirt, smell it as he breathed, and didn't care.

The last of the bugle notes died away and the RPD ceased firing. From the trees came a rising shout as the VC leaped from cover and raced across the open ground toward the burning hamlet. The flooded rice paddies made a perfect moat, slowing the enemy attack. If there had been a real defensive force, they would have had the opportunity to cut the Vietcong to ribbons.

But there wasn't. There were only two frightened men with outdated weapons they didn't understand, waiting to die.

Nguyen Van Vo aimed his bolt-action rifle at the nearest Vietcong soldier and gently pulled the trigger as he had been taught. The weapon fired, slamming back into his shoulder, causing him pain. He worked the bolt, ejecting the spent cartridge and aimed a second time. But he didn't flinch as the rifle fired and he saw one of the Vietcong stumble and fall. The dying soldier tossed his AK out in front of him, stretching out his hands as he disappeared into the muck and water of the rice paddy.

The enemy began shooting from their hips, as they ran toward the hamlet, at first only a couple of them, and then the whole assault force. The incoming rounds forced Vo to put his head down. His movements were slow, as if he was unimpressed by the enemy, but once he was crouched behind the ruined bunker he froze. He clutched the weapon in his left hand as he listened to the crack of rounds passing over his head.

To the right his companion was whimpering, and Vo could smell the fear emanating from the man's body. A tangible odor of sweat and excrement as the man lost his dignity, becoming no more than a frightened, defenseless animal.

Firing tapered off as the Vietcong reached the edge of the hamlet. The officers were shouting orders to the assault force. A squad broke from the main body, running across the open ground and leaping the last few feet that separated them from the two defenders.

Vo looked up in time to see the enemy seize Vo's frightened codefender, jerking him to his feet. They punched and kicked him and he cried out in pain. When he sagged, they yanked him up, hitting him in the face, chest and stomach. Blood covered his face and he spit broken teeth.

One of the Vietcong, a big man with a huge knife, stepped in front of the beaten defender. With a single stroke, he slit the man from crotch to sternum. The man shrieked, his voice high-pitched, like tires on dry concrete. The soldiers let go of his arms, and he clutched at his stomach, trying to keep his intestines from cascading to the dirt. He dropped to his knees, then sprawled forward on the steaming mass and lay still.

Now the attackers turned their attention to Vo. He snapped up his rifle and fired, but the shot was wild. The enemy didn't shoot back. They leaped at him and knocked him over, punching at him. One of the assailants ripped Vo's rifle from his hands. Caught off balance, he pressed his palm into the dirt to support himself. A boot came crashing down onto his fingers. He heard the bones snap and felt the white-hot pain from his hand flash up his arm to his shoulder. He was suddenly sick to his stomach.

Before he had time to retch, Vo felt himself jerked to his feet, and he knew they were going to cut open his stomach and dance on his entrails. But that didn't happen. Two men held his arms while a third held an ankle. Using a long metal rod, the leader struck him until he broke a leg.

Vo watched with detached interest. It was almost as if the torture was happening to someone else. He heard the thud of the blow, sounding like a bat against a sandbag and he heard the snap of the bone as it finally broke, but there was no pain. Shock had wiped that out.

They repeated the process on the other leg and then dropped him to the ground, letting him lie there. He could feel the hot blood on his legs and he felt something warm at his crotch. His hand throbbed and he still thought he was going to be sick. Although the Vietcong had left him without a guard, he had no desire to move. He knew he couldn't summon the energy to run even had it been possible on broken legs.

There was shouting from the center of the hamlet, men screaming commands, women wailing and children whimpering. Single shots were fired into the air as the people were herded from their hiding places. The hootches were torched as the villagers evacuated them.

After everyone was gathered in the center of the hamlet, the VC searched the hootches that weren't burning, stealing everything they wanted and smashing everything they didn't. In the course of their search they found an additional twelve rifles, obviously belonging to men who had been members of the local defense force.

That infuriated the Vietcong leader. He stormed through the hamlet, demanding the names of the men who owned the weapons. He cursed and spit, punching women and children as he stomped through the crowd. He raved against the cowardly Americans and their puppet soldiers. He denounced the Vietnamese who would help the Americans, and threatened to shoot everyone in the village if they didn't give him the names of the men who owned the weapons.

When no one surrendered the names, he separated twelve men from the group at random, pushing them against the wall of the concrete arms locker that the Americans had built. He lined up a squad of men facing the prisoners, ordered them to aim and fire.

The bursts ripped through the night. The bullets smashed into the men, who performed jerky little dances before slumping to the ground. When they were lying in the dirt, the Vietcong officer moved among them, cutting each throat just in case the bullets had failed to kill everyone.

The stunned villagers could do nothing. They didn't move or speak, staring awestruck at the bloody bodies of the dead men.

The VC assault force moved through the hamlet, setting everything on fire that wasn't already burning. They then forced a number of the older boys and girls to join them— children who were no more than thirteen or fourteen.

The Vietcong gathered at the edge of the hamlet, looking back at the destruction. Roaring flames leaped into the sky. Every structure either was on fire or had been destroyed by the mortar and rocket attack. The buildings that the Americans had been so proud of, the school and the dispensary, were rubble. The sanitation system designed to drain the standing water from the hamlet was destroyed, and the sandbags erected around hootches to protect the people had been slashed. The VC had even tried to smash the bricks and cinder blocks used for the buildings so that they couldn't be rebuilt. Bodies lay near the concrete arms locker; some lay scattered through the hamlet where they had fallen as the mortars exploded, or were lying at the edge of its perimeter.

Vo watched the Vietcong begin to retreat from the hamlet, slipping into the rice paddies to the east. They were dragging the children, whose arms were bound behind their backs. Vo tried to shut out the cries of anguish from the mothers who knew they were never going to see their offspring again. From the center of the hamlet where there had been sporadic rifle shots came the sounds of more sobbing. Vo knew that the Vietcong had executed those who had resisted, even if the resistance was a stare of hatred.

But he felt a surge of elation. He was still alive. Maybe the Vietcong weren't going to kill him. They had forgotten about him. Maybe they were going to let him live as a reminder to the others.

The VC leader broke off from his company and walked toward Vo. He seemed even bigger than before. In his agony, Vo noted that the officer wore the black pajamas of the Vietcong, but he also had a pistol, underscoring his status as an officer.

He crouched next to Vo and gently lifted his head, like a medic about to treat a wounded soldier. He stared down into Vo's eyes. "You see the power of the People's Army. You see what we can do?"

Vo nodded slowly. His lips and mouth were dry so that it was hard for him to speak. "I see" was all that he could manage to say. He wanted water but was afraid to ask for it, fearing he would anger the Vietcong officer.

"The Americans and the puppet soldiers did nothing to help you here tonight. They throw you away like so much garbage. They flee to the brightness of the cities to be with whores. They corrupt and taint and then try to fix it with their stacks of worthless paper money. They care nothing for the Vietnamese people.''

In that moment, Vo believed everything the man was saying. He had, after all, seen the Americans flee the hamlet. He'd seen the scramble by the ARVN as they fought to catch up with the Americans.

"You are right, Comrade," said Vo, feeling his strength failing him. There was a tingling in his legs now as the feeling began to return. The shock of the injuries was beginning to wear off.

The Vietcong leader grinned. He had bad teeth and there was stubble on his chin. His breath smelled of fish and *noucmam*.

"Then you know why I do what I must do. It is because of the Americans and their puppets. It is because you have embraced the Americans and their puppets. It is something that you have brought on yourself."

Vo closed his eyes as the pain began anew, spreading throughout his broken body. "I understand," he said, not understanding at all, but afraid of what was going to happen next.

Gently, the Vietcong officer laid Vo's head on the ground. When Vo didn't open his eyes, the officer drew his pistol slowly and touched the barrel to Vo's forehead. Before the **wounded man could react, the officer pulled the trigger once.** The bullet shattered Vo's skull, blew out the rear of his head as it turned his brain to mush, and killed him in a single, blinding flash. Vo never knew what hit him.

The officer stood and holstered his weapon, then brushed the palms of his hands together quickly, as if trying to remove dust. He glanced at the dead man, his face distorted and his blood pooling rapidly under the smashed skull.

"A lesson for everyone," said the officer. He then turned and hurried after the last of his assault company, which was now almost to the trees.

1

**OUTSIDE THE HAMLET
OF DUC BANG,
REPUBLIC OF VIETNAM**

Lieutenant Kenneth Helmsman crouched at the corner of the rice paddy dike, the butt of his M-16 touching the dirty water. His boots were wet, as were the cuffs of his bright green fatigues. He was sweating heavily, the perspiration staining his underarms, his back and his waist. The steel pot he wore seemed excessively heavy, as did the flak jacket and the bandoliers of M-16 ammo. He had four grenades attached to his harness in the best tradition of the Hollywood soldier along with a Case combat knife taped upside down, and three canteens, one filled with Kool-Aid and the others filled with water.

Helmsman was a young man fresh from college. He had studied military tactics and science for four years, and had attended two six-week summer camps. Afterward he had managed to get jump training, and then entered the service, going to the Infantry Officers School at Fort Benning. But none of that had prepared him for command of an infantry platoon in the jungles of Vietnam. Fortunately, he had a sergeant who'd been in-country for six months and had a feel for what was going on.

Sergeant Paul Warren was even younger than Helmsman, but by Army standards, which counted time in-country, Warren was the old man, the professional soldier who would keep the men from getting killed as they learned the business of soldiering in Vietnam.

To the casual observer, the two men could have been brothers. Both were tall and reed-thin, though Helmsman had blond hair and blue eyes, while Warren's were dark. Warren was deeply tanned and Helmsman was burned pink, with peeling skin that didn't seem to ever tan. Warren had a series of small scars on his face and neck from a Chicom grenade that had exploded close to him with only enough force to cut him up without doing too much damage.

Helmsman wanted to sit down on the rice paddy dike, lift his feet from the muddy, filth-laden water, but refused to do so. He was trying hard to set an example for the men who were more interested in going home than in dying for the Vietnamese. Helmsman thought about how nice it would be to have a bath, a shave and a clean uniform. Instead, he stood under the blazing tropical sun, sweating heavily, and smelling bad from three days in the field without benefit of bath or razor. The lack of a bath, Warren had told him, was a good thing. It kept the insects from biting too often. It also kept the Vietcong from finding him because of his after-shave or deodorant. Now he smelled like the jungle.

Glancing to his left, he saw the RTO, the radio telephone operator, crouched in another paddy. He was holding on to the antenna, bending it down over his shoulder so that it wasn't sticking in the air like some kind of aiming stake. Warren had told Helmsman to stay away from the RTO as much as possible, because NVA snipers liked to shoot the men clustered around them.

The rest of the platoon was spread out in line, using the short dikes for cover as they surveyed the still-smoking ruins of the hamlet of Duc Bang. They were also young men, plucked from high schools and colleges. They were men who screwed around too much, drank too much beer, had too much fun and ended up failing too many courses. Young men without the financial backing to hide in college regardless of grades, or to find a friendly doctor who would claim high blood pressure or fallen arches. Now they were all grim-faced young men waiting for their sergeant and their lieutenant to order them forward to flush the enemy.

Helmsman finally took a step forward over the dike. He wanted to take off his helmet and wipe the sweat from his face, but knew better than that. He touched his lips and then cheeks with the back of his hand and started moving. He didn't point, wave the men forward or shout orders. Warren had already warned him about that. He just started forward slowly, glancing right and left to make sure the platoon was preparing to follow.

The hamlet squatted on a slight plateau, maybe eight or nine feet above the surrounding countryside. Smoke hung over it like an early-morning mist. The only movement was from a huge black bird that squawked and ran along the ground near what had once been the bunker line. The hootches and bunkers were empty shells.

They were fifty yards from the hamlet when the staccato burst of machine-gun fire ripped through the afternoon. Helmsman didn't look at his men. He dived to the ground, landing on his belly in eighteen inches of water. If he hadn't known before how the rice paddies were fertilized, he understood then. The stench filled his nostrils and made him gag. For a moment he forgot about the enemy machine gun as he tried to keep his lunch down.

There was shouting on the right and answering fire from two M-16s. Helmsman's first instinct was the one that he'd been taught at the infantry school. Charge the ambush. But that was in the jungle, where the two forces were separated by three or four yards at the most. To charge the machine gun nest here, they would have to cover fifty or sixty yards of open ground. Suicide, Helmsman thought.

Warren was on his knees behind a dike in an awkward posture. He was firing his weapon on full-automatic, aiming into the jungle where the machine gun seemed to be situated.

One of the men was lying on his back, holding his M-79 grenade launcher over his body, pointing toward the jungle behind his head. He had his thumb on the trigger, the barrel over his face. A corporal crouched in the corner of the dike was trying to direct the fire. When the round fell, he shouted orders at the grenadier, who broke open the weapon and reloaded, never moving from his position on his back.

Helmsman crawled toward the RTO, who held the handset against his ear, but was saying nothing. Helmsman got to him and snapped his fingers, holding out his hand. When the RTO surrendered the handset, Helmsman said, "Get me the closest arty advisory."

The RTO changed the frequency and said, "You got it, sir. Duc Hoa."

"Duc Hoa arty, Duc Hoa arty, this is Black Raider one six, I have a fire mission, over."

"Black Raider one six, this is Duc Hoa arty, go."

Helmsman twisted around, pulling his map from his pocket. It had been covered with acetate, but the rice paddy water had gotten to it. It was a fragile soggy mess, but he could still read the coordinates and that was good enough.

Duc Bang was at the center of the section he had been looking at since the morning before the patrol. He studied the area on the map, looking for landmarks. The enemy fire was coming from a tree line. According to the map, it was a half klick from the hamlet, but that didn't look quite right.

Helmsman squeezed the handset and fed the coordinates over the radio to the arty advisory. He didn't use a code, but gave them in the clear, hoping that the enemy, if they were monitoring the right freq, would get out.

The arty advisory repeated the coordinates, then said, "Shot, over."

"Shot, out," said Helmsman.

Around him, his platoon was firing steadily into the trees. Some of the men were shooting on full-auto, burning through their ammo and then ducking down to reload. Others were using short bursts or single shot. The overall effect was a rippling, ragged volley that poured into the trees but failed to silence the enemy machine gunners.

Helmsman worried about mortars. If it was a sizable enemy unit, they would have mortars, but so far none had fallen. The only artillery was the M-79 grenade launcher, blooping out the rounds that the spotter called for. They were falling short, but it kept the two men busy.

Then, overhead, was the warbling rush of an oncoming freight train. There was a massive explosion and the ground short of the tree line erupted into a brown-silver geyser.

Helmsman squeezed the handset. "Add one hundred and right one hundred."

"Shot over."

"Shot, out."

A moment later, the second round smashed into the ground among the trees. Helmsman spotted the orange flash of the detonation and the smoke rising through the trees. It appeared to be close to the enemy weapon.

"On target. Fire for effect."

"Rounds on the way."

The barrage landed among the tress. The series of detonations threw dirt and dust and bits of vegetation into the air. Red-hot shrapnel cut through the finger of jungle, slamming into trees, cutting off branches. A dust cloud formed over the canopy, drifting to the east slowly on the light afternoon breeze.

"Last rounds on the way," said the man at the arty advisory.

"Last rounds," repeated Helmsman.

There were a final six detonations and then it was suddenly, eerily quiet. Helmsman's platoon had quit firing and the RPD hidden in the trees was silent. He waited for a few seconds and then waved an arm over his head to motion his men forward. He was on his feet, loping toward smoking trees. At the edge of the tree line Helmsman threw himself to the ground. On either side of him, his men did the same, their weapons held at the ready, but there was no enemy fire.

For a moment he held there, listening. No sounds from the monkeys that normally inhabited the forest. No birds windmilling overhead and no buzzing of insects. All the little background sounds were missing. Helmsman couldn't help thinking of the movie cliché, "It's too quiet, I don't like it."

But this time, it wasn't because there was an ambush waiting. It was the result of the artillery. The cannon cockers at Duc Hoa had silenced the machine gun, but they had also silenced the animals that lived in the forest, and that worried Helmsman. Even in his brief experience he'd come to trust the sounds of the jungle.

Warren crawled toward him. His uniform was now a mess, stained with mud and soaked with water from the paddies so that it looked black. Dirt was smeared on his face, but Helmsman suspected Warren had done that himself, trying to cover the brightest parts of his white skin.

"Think they di-di-ed," said Warren, meaning that he believed the enemy had fled.

"We've got to sweep through there anyway," said Helmsman. "Arty wants a body count and Saigon won't be happy without one."

"Yes, sir," said Warren. He slowly got to his feet and crouched at the edge of the trees, staring into the darkness of the jungle, deep greens and blacks with patches of sunlight filtering through. The dust hung heavy in the air, the faint breeze doing nothing to blow it away.

The platoon got to its feet and the men filtered into the tree line, watching right, left and ahead. They moved carefully, their weapons ready because the enemy had been there. The RPD had proved that.

After ten minutes, Helmsman was beginning to think that they had fulfilled their obligation to the cannon cockers. They had found nothing and they still had to sweep through the hamlet of Duc Bang.

"Over here!" shouted Sergeant Warren.

Helmsman worked his way through the trees and vegetation, avoiding the wait-a-minute vines that tore at his uniform and skin. There were other vines wrapped around the trunks of trees, slowly squeezing the life from them. And there were broken and splintered branches, the result of the artillery. Bark had been stripped from the trees and some of the trunks looked shattered. Wisps of smoke curled up from a few of the broken trees. Shrapnel, that would slowly kill them, was embedded in their trunks.

Warren was standing near a crater created when a shell exploded. He held a length of metal in his hand as if it was a trophy fish.

"RPD barrel," he said. "Looks like the round hit them direct. That's what I call calling in the arty. Right on the fucking target."

"Bodies?" asked Helmsman.

"Don't be ridiculous. We find anything, it's going to be a small piece. We can count two dead. The gunner and the assistant. The RPD tells us that much."

Helmsman got closer. "How do you know that hasn't been lying out here for a week?"

"Metal's too bright. If it had been lying out here, the elements would have gotten to it. Besides, the Vietnamese wouldn't let something like this go to waste. Someone would have carted it off."

Helmsman stared into the crater, trying to spot the remains of the men who had been behind the gun, but they were gone. Warren was right. They'd get credit for at least two enemy KIA. The way Saigon was inflating the body counts, they might get more, he thought wryly.

"Nothing else to do here. Let's get the men formed and head toward the hamlet."

"Yes, sir."

The platoon retreated from the tree line, three of them dropping back as a rear guard. Once everyone was clear of the trees, the three men joined the squad on the sweep toward Duc Bang.

Everyone stayed off the paddy dikes, afraid that the Vietcong might have booby-trapped them. In many areas, the Vietcong avoided doing that because the people killed and injured would be farmers and not soldiers. But this was a strategic hamlet. The enemy would do anything possible to disrupt life there and force the inhabitants from it.

The platoon crossed the open ground, using the paddies, stepping on the young plants so that their feet didn't sink into the muck at the bottoms of the paddies. They came to the end of the fields and to dry ground. Now it was possible to see the ruins around them. Bunkers blown apart, the remains still smoking slightly. The interior of the hamlet didn't have a single structure that wasn't damaged.

And as they got close, they heard the buzzing of flies. On the breeze came the odor of death. Bodies that had been burned and bodies that had lain in the sun.

The patrol fanned out, checking the structures for the enemy, searching for the villagers. Helmsman and Warren found them huddled in the remains of the arms locker. Outside it were the bodies of a dozen men who had been machine-gunned. Their blood had turned the ground a rusty color, not much different from the natural earth of Vietnam. Flies were hovering over the bodies, the buzzing sounding unnaturally loud. A lone dog lay in the shade, watching the dead men, almost as if guarding them.

As they rounded the corner, they found the old women and men and the children. They sat huddled in the corner of the now roofless bunker, their eyes wide with fear. None of them spoke or moved.

Helmsman handed his M-16 to Warren and then stepped down into the locker. He crouched, holding out a hand in a gesture of friendship. In a quiet voice he said, "We're here. We've come to help."

There was no response and he looked back over his shoulder to where Warren stood. "Go find the medic and get him over here. Collect the C-rats from the men and bring them."

"Security, Lieutenant."

"Of course. See to that."

Warren shrugged. "Yes, sir."

Helmsman turned his attention back to the people in the locker. Fifteen or twenty people jammed together, as if using one another for protection.

"Where are the others?" asked Helmsman. There was no response. It was as if he wasn't even there. Their faces were blank. They were in another world.

He moved forward and crouched immediately in front of them. The eyes of a girl followed him but the rest of the people didn't acknowledge him.

There was a sound behind him and the medic stood there. "What do you need, Lieutenant?"

Helmsman waved a hand. "Check these people out and see if there's anything you can do for them."

"Yes, sir."

The medic moved in and stooped. He touched the head of a girl. She looked at him but didn't move, telling him that he could do anything to her that he wanted, that nothing could be worse than the horror of the night before.

"We're here to help you," said Helmsman again.

"Where were you last night?" asked a quiet, accusing female voice.

SPECIAL FORCES CAPTAIN Mackenzie Gerber sat at a small white table on the sidewalk outside the Continental Hotel in the area known locally as the Continental Shelf. He was dressed in clean jungle fatigues, new jungle boots and a new beret. He held a copy of the *Stars and Stripes*, reading about the results of the Tet offensive.

On the table in front of him were a glass of orange juice and the remains of his breakfast. He had ordered a large one because somehow he and Robin Morrow had never gotten dinner eaten the night before. He had awakened early, nearly starving, and had made his way down to the Shelf.

Gerber was in his mid-thirties. He had brown hair and blue eyes. He was a tall, slender man who had been described as lean and mean. After several weeks in the tropics, he was deeply tanned and no longer found the climate as stifling as it had been when he arrived in November. In the World, it had been cold, rainy and windy. Here it was hot and muggy, and he hadn't been ready for the temperature change. But out here, in the middle of Saigon, he was sitting in the shadows and there was a light breeze blowing on him. It was actually comfortable, a rare occurrence in Saigon.

Gerber turned the page and folded the paper back on itself. He then folded it in half and set it on the table so that he could read and still keep his hands free. Lifting his gaze off the page, he took the opportunity to study the people around him. They were mainly civilians, dressed for the tropics in white suits or khaki safari outfits. The few women, employees of the embassy or the local news service bureaus, wore short skirts and light blouses. They had only recently returned to Saigon after the Tet attacks.

The men all had the same leering look about them. Away from the wife and family, they were chasing the younger women. Gerber grinned to himself and then returned to his newspaper.

A shadow fell across his table and he looked up into the face of Master Sergeant Anthony B. Fetterman. Fetterman, dressed in new fatigues, was a small man with thinning hair, a dark complexion and a heritage he claimed included the Aztec and the Sioux. He had shaved recently, but Gerber knew that to meet military regulations, he'd have to shave again about the middle of the afternoon. He had been in the Army for more than twenty years, parachuting into France as a teenager, and probably knew more about soldiering than any two other soldiers Gerber could name. A true professional in every sense of the word.

"Morning, Captain."

"Morning, Master Sergeant."

Fetterman slipped into a vacant chair. "Miss Morrow not with you today?"

"Miss Morrow is sleeping. She didn't seem to get much sleep last night, though I can't figure out what might have kept her awake." Gerber put his paper away. "You going to have breakfast?"

"No, sir. I ate earlier this morning. I came to find you because we're wanted over at MACV Headquarters about an hour from now."

Gerber stared at him. "You're always appearing on my doorstep with the news that someone wants us somewhere in an very short period of time. It's getting to be an old story and one I'm tired of hearing."

"Yes, sir," said Fetterman.

"You're going to have to move out of those NCO quarters at Tan Son Nhut. Makes it too easy to find you on these last-minute exercises. If they can't find you, then they go off to find someone else."

Fetterman didn't speak. He merely nodded.

"They can't find me," continued Gerber, "because I move around and I stay out of the quarters provided for us. A moving target is harder to hit."

"I have a jeep," said Fetterman.

Gerber laughed. "You always have a jeep."

"I figure you have enough time for another cup of coffee if you want it," said Fetterman. "Morning traffic's thinned out some by now."

"I'm not interested in another cup of coffee. I'm not particularly interested in a meeting over at MACV. What I want to do is sit here and read the newspaper, sip my juice and forget about nearly everything else."

"Well," said Fetterman, "those are the orders."

Robin Morrow appeared then, looking as if she hadn't been awake for very long. Her blond hair had been combed but wasn't perfect. She had a trace of makeup on, but it had been hastily applied and smudged slightly. Her green eyes were barely open and yet she was the best-looking woman around. Tall and slim, she wore a light yellow sundress with a plunging neckline and a short hem. But she didn't look very cool. Before either Gerber or Fetterman could stand, she sat down and growled, "I want coffee. I need coffee."

"Then we'd better get you some," said Fetterman.

"Good morning, Robin," said Gerber.

"What in the hell did you do to me last night?" she asked. "I didn't think I'd be able to get out of bed and I feel like I've been hit by a tank."

"You look very nice," said Fetterman.

She bowed in his direction. "Thank you, Master Sergeant. I see there is one gentleman at the table. That doesn't include the one who is supposed to be an officer and a gentleman."

"I believe," said Gerber, taking on the tones of a college professor lecturing a class of slow students, "that we are now just officers and no longer gentlemen. Congress decided they couldn't force us to be gentlemen."

"Well, that figures," said Morrow.

"Tony and I have to head over to MACV in a little while for some kind of meeting."

She waved a hand as she yawned. "Go. I should get to work anyway before they forget what I look like." She didn't look up.

"Well," said Gerber, "I'll buy you a cup of coffee and then Tony and I have to punch out of here."

"And I'll see you for dinner?"

"Sure," said Gerber. "Why not?"

2

MACV HEADQUARTERS SAIGON, REPUBLIC OF VIETNAM

Both Gerber and Fetterman sat in the second rank of chairs with the other junior officers and NCOs. In front of them were the colonels and generals and politicians who were going to dictate policy. The table was highly polished and glowed a deep brown. A tea service sat in the center of the table, the sides of the pitcher beaded with moisture. At one end was a covered easel, and a sergeant in fatigues stood at attention near it as if guarding it.

The men around the table were all dressed in khakis or suits, making it look like a boardroom where they were discussing a military procurement contract. The high-backed chairs were covered in leather.

The air-conditioning hummed quietly, blowing cool air at them from vents hidden near the ceiling. The breeze tugged at the huge American flag in the corner. Gerber noticed that there was no South Vietnamese flag in the room. There were no South Vietnamese personnel there, either.

Gerber leaned over and whispered to Fetterman. "What in the hell is this all about?"

"Who knows, sir?"

Before he could speak again, the door opened and another general, along with two civilians, entered. Someone announced the commander and everyone got to his feet. The newcomers took their places at the head of the table. As the general sat down, he said, "Please be seated."

Once everyone was comfortable again and the rustling had stopped, the general began. "For those of you who don't know me, I'm General Thomas H. Padgett. I'm deputy commander for civilian strategic affairs. I've been overseeing the strategic hamlet concept as it has been developed here for the past several months." He waved a hand. "Everyone understand that? Any questions about that?"

When no one spoke, Padgett turned toward the sergeant and the easel and snapped his fingers. The sergeant drew the cloth off it and then stepped aside. There was a map of the Three Corps area with a number of hamlets marked in black. Most were near the Cambodian border, where they would be useful in interdicting the traffic along the Ho Chi Minh Trail.

"Captain Collins, can you give us an update on the status of the strategic hamlet operation?"

Collins stood in the second row and moved forward to the easel. Like most of the generals and colonels, Collins was dressed in a khaki uniform. He was a short, stocky man with a bald spot on the back of his head, a slight paunch and pink skin. He didn't seem to have spent much time out in the sun, and if he had been walking down a street in civilian clothes, he would have looked more like a college teacher than he did a military officer.

He nodded at the easel and the sergeant removed the first map. On the second was a stylized drawing of a hamlet. It was oval shaped, had squares that marked the buildings and labels stuck on to identify the structures. Collins took a pointer and tucked it under his arm as if it was a swagger stick.

"This is Duc Bang, a small hamlet in War Zone C near Tay Ninh City. It was constructed by American forces using a plan developed at MACV Headquarters. At one point, there were fifty Americans and a company of ARVN stationed in the hamlet. Now, given the requirements of the Tet defense, all American soldiers have been pulled from the village and returned to their units during our operations in the past few weeks. I understand that the ARVN forces also left."

One of the men in the front row asked, "Were they ordered out as were our troops?" He was one of the civilians, and gave the impression that he hadn't been in the tropics for very long.

"We believe that the pullout of the American forces precipitated the withdrawal of the ARVN. In other words, they scrammed when the Americans left."

"So there were no regular forces in the hamlet," said the man.

"Strictly speaking, no," answered Collins. "There was an internal defense force developed among the locals, and weapons were left for their use."

"How did they do?" asked the man.

"Please, we're getting ahead of ourselves here," said Collins. "I'll answer all your questions if you'll give me a chance. I'm sure some of them will be covered in the course of my briefing." He moved forward and used the pointer, snapping it against the easel as he spoke. He explained that the concept was a good one, noting that the plan was to teach the locals to defend themselves from the Communists. It was a plan aimed at thwarting the VC at their own game. The concept was designed to provide the Vietnamese with the ability to resist the Communists, and it was a concept that would allow the Americans to reduce their participation in protecting the innocent civilians.

"Then what went wrong at—" the civilian flipped a hand toward the easel "—Duc Bang?"

"Nothing went wrong," said Collins. "We were forced to redeploy our forces before they could complete their training and the construction of their hamlet. The locals were tested before they had the chance to be properly prepared."

"Oh-oh," whispered Fetterman, leaning close to Gerber. "Here it comes."

"But something happened," said the man, grinning in triumph. "If it hadn't, we wouldn't be here."

"Radio reports received earlier today suggest that a small VC force hit the hamlet in the past twenty-four hours and killed a number of the inhabitants," said Collins.

"How many?" asked the civilian.

"That information is not available, as the sweep of the hamlet has not been completed."

"I was concerned about the number of Vietcong soldiers."

"Current intelligence estimates suggest the VC have accomplished their mission and have withdrawn from the area. There are no more VC in the area."

Padgett sensed that Collins was getting in over his head. The civilian was directing the conversation, taking control away from the captain. Padgett nodded then and said, "Thank you, Captain. Now our plan is to rebuild the hamlet right where it stands. The foundation has already been constructed. Some of the villagers escaped and there are hundreds of refugees from the Communist invasion that would jump at the chance to have a nice home and a few acres to farm. They will be used to repopulate the hamlet." He pointed to one of the civilians who sat in the second row.

The man stood, nodded self-consciously and began to speak in a quiet, almost inaudible voice. He hadn't bothered to move to the front where the easel stood. Padgett snapped his fingers and said, "Speak up, Doctor."

"Yes, quite." He then moved to the vacated place at the side of the easel. "Gentlemen, it seems that we have been given a very delicate problem here. We need to defeat the enemy without wasting an extraordinary amount of our resources in the process. Billions of dollars could be poured into the Vietnam conflict without any tangible results."

"No shit," whispered someone in the back.

The speaker elected not to hear the comment and went right on. "Now, this strategic hamlet idea is one that is workable, if we put our minds to it and don't let ourselves get sidetracked by trivia. We must commit to it and see it through. The Communist offensive did that—sidetracked us. Now we need to put our train back on the track."

"Please be brief, Doctor," said Padgett.

"Certainly, General." He waved a hand in the air, almost as if hailing a cab. "What we want to do is build these hamlets, little islands of resistance throughout Vietnam. Use Duc Bang as the model, especially since the VC have shown an interest in it, and then continue to build. Control the countryside that way. Give the people the opportunity to grow their food and deny it to the Communists. In time, the VC will have no support in the fields and they will be forced to capitulate."

"Meaning?" asked Fetterman.

"Meaning, obviously," said the doctor, "that we have to reestablish the hamlet that was burned by the Communists and repopulate it. Prove to the enemy that a minor setback is not going to disrupt our plan. Show the Communists that we are committed to this concept. At the same time, we show the locals that we are willing to aid them in this activity."

There were questions that Fetterman wanted to ask, but he had already trampled on military protocol and courtesy by shouting out his question. Instead he leaned over and said to Gerber, "Here it comes, sir. Right at us."

"Relax," said Gerber. "We don't know that."

Fetterman shook his head. "There's no other reason for us to be sitting here."

Gerber had no answer to that. He was afraid that the master sergeant was right.

As if to confirm what they feared, the doctor smiled and looked pointedly at Gerber and Fetterman. "Our friends in the Special Forces are particularly suited for this sort of work. The A-detachments scattered throughout Vietnam have established the types of islands in the sea of Communist domination that I have been speaking about. Now, rather than creating tiny American states, we want to create tiny Vietnamese states, at first under American protection, to resist the Communist infiltration."

One of the colonels interrupted. "Then you're telling us that we should never have abandoned that hamlet in the first place."

"Exactly. We've made our task just that much harder, but looking at this from a purely scientific point of view, we can recover the lost ground quickly. We teach the Vietnamese in these hamlets how to defend themselves and we have our strategic hamlet intact."

"Never work," said Fetterman under his breath. "Farmers do not make good soldiers."

But the men at the table weren't concerned with that. Orders had been issued in Washington, D.C., to be implemented in South Vietnam, and the American press, stunned by the immediate gains of the Vietcong and the North Vietnamese, were already suggesting that the military had been lying. Vietnamization, a term that had been used only in the innermost circles, was now being talked about in the open. One way to end the problem was to have the Vietnamese take over a large portion of the war. The strategic hamlets fit into that concept very nicely.

So the discussion wasn't about the feasibility of the strategic hamlets and teaching farmers to be soldiers. It was about how fast they could put men into the field and how much support they would need. Finally one of the colonels, a man who haunted the inner corridors of MACV Headquarters, turned and pointed at Gerber. Gerber had seen the man a dozen times, but had never spoken to him.

"General, Captain Gerber, whom we ordered to be here this morning, had command of an A-team at one time and has worked with the people."

Padgett looked at Gerber and asked, "What do you think of all this?"

Gerber shrugged and parroted Fetterman's words. "You can't turn farmers into soldiers."

"Come now, Captain," said Padgett, "we do it all the time. The citizen soldier is the backbone of the American military machine."

"Yes, sir," said Gerber. "We take young men, nineteen, twenty years old, who have a knowledge of our technology, who have knowledge of weapons, and teach them to be soldiers. But we also have a solid core of NCOs and officers who are professionals. The difference is that you want us to take men and women who have no knowledge of technology, who may never have seen a rifle, and teach them to defend themselves without benefit of any trained officer or NCO infrastructure."

"I understand that, Captain," said Padgett. "But I'm afraid I don't understand your reluctance to take on this mission."

"I didn't know a mission had been assigned," said Gerber.

"Let's not mince words, Captain. Obviously a mission is going to be assigned. There is no other rationale for you to be here. Do you object for some unstated reason?"

"Excuse me, General, but I didn't say I wouldn't do this, I merely said we might be expecting results that are impossible to obtain. You want to take thirty-, forty- and fifty-year-old men and women and teach them to be soldiers. The task is going to be much harder than everyone expects it to be."

"What do you need?" asked Padgett.

Gerber rubbed his face as he thought. "The first thing that comes to mind is put a Special Forces A-detachment into the hamlet and let them handle the problem. Give them the help, the supplies they need and let them have a go at it."

"How soon can you get your men into the field?" asked Padgett.

Gerber fought the urge to snap at the man. Instead, he looked at the blank faces at the table, at the military officers who had built their careers by staying off the firing line and never questioning their superiors, and at civilians who had been promoted because they were good at agreeing. If he agreed, he knew that he could be cutting his own throat.

"General," he said, "I have no A-detachment and am assigned to MACV-SOG. Our mission is somewhat different than that of the A-detachments."

"Well," said Padgett, smiling, "your assignment has just been changed and you will put together an A-detachment to hit the field no later than tomorrow morning. Any questions?"

Gerber had a dozen, but knew that he could ask none of them. His orders had been issued and there were so many witnesses here, they would have to be obeyed. The only thing he could do was set up the team, hit the field and then work on extracting himself from what he was convinced was a futile assignment.

"No, General," said Gerber. "No questions. Only where do I find the men."

WHEN GERBER AND FETTERMAN left the Continental Shelf, Robin Morrow sat at the white rattan table and sipped her coffee. Her head ached, her stomach was churning and she saw double. It was almost as bad as a hangover, and she hadn't even had the fun of drinking. It was the result of a lack of sleep.

She held the cup in her shaking hands, inches from her nose, and inhaled the aroma as if she could gain strength from it. There was nothing about the night before that she regretted, except that it had lasted until first light. Then, lying on her back, the strength gone from her arms and legs and a light coating of perspiration covering her body, she had felt relaxed enough to sleep. A slow process after she had been numbed. She had never experienced anything like the lifting to the plateau and the sustaining activity. The night had been that rare combination of the right time and the right feelings and the right person. It had seemed that it would never end. And now she wasn't sure that she would survive.

Finally, feeling that she could now move again, she got to her feet and walked into the hotel. She crossed the lobby without seeing it. She was dimly aware that there were people around her but she paid no attention to them. She just walked straight to the elevator and gave the operator her floor.

In the tiny room, she sat on the rumpled bed. The covers and top sheet had been kicked to the floor and they hadn't bothered retrieving them. Gerber's dirty uniform was lying on the floor, too, as was some of his equipment. There was an extra canteen and a first-aid kit on a pistol belt.

Morrow's clothes were scattered around the room. In their haste they'd somehow managed to remove her dress without damaging it, but her panties had gotten torn. She didn't remember how as she picked the scrap of cloth off the floor. But then they had been so fragile that it wasn't surprising.

Finally, she got up and walked into the bathroom. A giant tub stood on clawed feet. There was a rust stain where the faucet dripped and a plug on a chain to keep the water from running out, but it was a real bathtub and the water would be hot.

She stripped out of her clothes, dropped them to the floor, then leaned over the tub and turned on the water. She added some bubble bath, which had been given to her by a man who worked at the embassy. She tested the water once, turned on the cold and then let the tub fill. While it did, she looked at herself in the mirror. Sucking in her breath, she turned from side to side, her head held high.

It was a good body, she decided. Maybe her breasts were too small, but they didn't sag and there wasn't an ounce of fat on her. A firm, athletic body. She turned again, looking at her backside and then at her back. If she had a single flaw, it was her back. There was a network of tiny scars on it, a gift from a Vietcong officer. She rarely thought about it now, and if she stayed out of the sun, the scars would fade so that they would be hardly noticeable.

She turned and stepped into the tub, the hot water swirling around her ankles and the bubbles nearly to her knees. She sat down and leaned back, letting the hot water wash over her, until it was up to her chin. Then, with her foot, she turned off the tap and just relaxed.

It was so comfortable in the bath that she nearly fell asleep. She let her mind drift, not concentrating on anything. A kaleidoscope of thoughts whirled through her head without direction. Moments of memory that were like frames cut from a hundred different movies.

And then the mood was broken. She sat up, her shoulders and chest covered with bubbles and glanced to the rear, at the door. There had been a noise in the hallway, but no one entered. Satisfied that she was still alone, she rinsed the soap from her body and got out of the tub, then snagged the chain and let the water escape. She toweled herself dry and walked into the bedroom.

Without conscious thought, she dressed, putting on a khaki-colored jumpsuit that had become her personal trademark. Rather than the baggy things that she had once worn, these were tailored to her body. There were more than enough tailors now that the Americans had arrived in force. The Vietnamese had adapted well to the influx of Americans.

She used to hack off the arms and legs of the jumpsuits, but now the tailor did that, too, hemming them so that it was a good-looking custom job. She'd turned more than one head and gotten more than one man to talk more freely than he realized.

Dressed, she grabbed her camera bag and left the room. She made her way downstairs and out into the humidity of the encroaching afternoon. For a moment she stood on the curb, watching the traffic flow. Hundreds of cars, jeeps, motorbikes and Lambrettas fought one another for space on the street. There were horns and whistles and shouts of anger. The noise seemed to build, whirling around like debris in a windstorm.

At that moment, Robin realized that she was happy. The night before had been wonderful, more than that, maybe even magnificent. She was doing an important job in Vietnam, telling the American people what was really happening, and her colleagues respected her for her talents, especially when she was the only one who had seen Tet coming. The others had thought the war over.

Rather than taking a cab, she turned and walked down the street. The bath had refreshed her and her aches were gone. Her head didn't hurt and even the heat of late morning didn't bother her. She accepted it now, as she did everything else about Vietnam. That was just the way it was.

She came to the press bureau, stood outside the door of the three-story white building and looked up at the facade. It was an old building, constructed by the French when they were trying to turn Saigon into the Paris of the Orient.

She pressed the button, identified herself to the tinny voice of a hidden speaker and heard the door buzz open. She entered and hurried up the narrow stairs. She walked down the hallway and entered the room that would have been the city arena if she had worked for a newspaper in the World. There was a sea of desks in front of her, those closest to the bank of windows at the front belonging to the senior people. To the right were a number of small offices that the editors used— glassed-in cages with only enough room for a desk, a visitor's chair and a bookcase.

Behind her along one wall were file cabinets that held little of importance. Almost no one used them. It was as if they had been put there in the same way that sandbags were stacked around a bunker.

Morrow walked to her desk, set her camera bag on the floor and sat down. She pulled at the middle drawer and then glanced to the right. Mark Hodges, her editor, had left his office and was walking toward her.

Hodges was a short, overweight man who was one of the few people who managed to gain weight while in Vietnam. It was a combination of huge lunches and bigger dinners and nights of drinking in the local night spots. He had black hair that was so heavily greased that he only had to comb it once a day. His pasty white skin was the result of staying inside as much as possible. He only ventured out of the air-conditioned comfort of his office, his hotel room or the bars and restaurants when he couldn't help it.

He parked a haunch on the corner of Morrow's desk and looked down at her, letting his eyes work their way from her ankles all the way up her body, lingering at her crotch and then chest, until he was staring at her face.

"Got an assignment for you if you're not working on anything else."

"I've nothing else," she said.

"Oh? You've spent so much time out of the office lately I thought you must have a big deal going."

Morrow wanted to tell him that she did have a big deal but that it had nothing to do with her search for a story. Instead she asked, "You got a problem with that?"

"No," said Hodges, shaking his head. "Just so long as you're around when I need you."

Morrow rocked back in her chair and propped her feet up on her desk, a green thing that had been given to the news bureau by the Army. She watched Hodges study her legs and then asked, "What have you got for me?"

"Little hamlet named, ah, something that's almost obscene, Duc something, Duc Bang, was hit by the Communists and overrun. Duc Bang, if you can believe it. Thought maybe you should take a look at it."

"Come on, Mark, that's no story. Hell, after Tet, the Communists overran a dozen, a hundred of these little villages as they swept through."

Hodges wiped a hand over his face and looked at the light coating of sweat. "I know that, but this one is special. Some kind of model village for the Vietnamese. I want you to go out there and take a look. Get a feel for the people's reaction to what happened to them. I need a big story that's well illustrated. Should be plenty of opportunities for good art on this."

She dropped her feet to the floor. "You want pictures of crying women staring at the dead bodies of their husbands and sons? Wailing upward as if calling to an unmerciful God? Maybe a little girl, sitting on the sand crying in the ruins of her village?"

"No reason to get sarcastic. Those pictures win prizes when the time comes." He held up a hand to stop the protest before it came. "What I want now is something about how the war affects these people. How it has changed their lives and what they do now to protect themselves."

"Okay," said Morrow. "I don't understand why you want this, but if that's what you're looking for, then I'll go out and do it. Now, where's this Duc Bang?"

"Out near the Cambodian border in War Zone C. Marvelous name that. Maybe we could work it into the headline somehow. Or make it the dateline. Dateline, War Zone C, Vietnam."

Morrow laughed. "I thought we were journalists, not novelists."

Hodges stood. "When you've got a great name, you work it into the story somehow. And that's the way it is." He laughed. "Come on into my office and I'll show you the map. Then we can see about getting you a ride out to the hamlet with the Army."

"Great," she said. "I can't wait."

3

INSIDE THE HAMLET OF
DUC BANG, WAR ZONE C
REPUBLIC OF VIETNAM

Helmsman ordered the surviving villagers out of the damaged arms locker, then had to issue threats to get them moving. They were a sullen lot, standing and walking as slowly as they could, almost like they were about to be executed. They stumbled into the sunlight, their eyes to the ground, as if the sight of the death and destruction around them was too much to bear.

The platoon had scattered through the hamlet, searching the ruined hootches and bunkers for wounded civilians, for weapons and for the enemy. Warren had broken off one squad as security, and they watched the surrounding countryside for signs that the VC or NVA were near.

Helmsman stopped the people, shouting at them. A few sank to the ground, their eyes closed. The medic moved among them, doing what he could for their injuries and burns. In ten minutes he had used almost all the medications and bandages he carried, and he hadn't done all that much.

"Some of these people are going to have to be evaced," he told Helmsman. "I can't do anything more for them. I don't have the supplies to take care of them."

"They in any real danger?"

"Not immediately, sir. Problem is infection. In this environment, the smallest wound can get infected and kill. I want them to get the antibiotics they need. Get the wounds cleansed, that sort of thing."

"You get me a list or, at the very least, the number of people who'll need to be evaced, and we'll see what we can do to get them out."

"Yes, sir." The medic bent back to his work, ignoring the cries of the children and the howls of outrage from some of the old men.

Helmsman pushed up the rim of his helmet so that the steel pot was seated on the back of his head. With the sleeve of his jungle fatigues he wiped the sweat from his face. He held his M-16 propped against his hip, his left hand on the pistol grip and the barrel angled into the air over his head. He watched his men searching the ruined hamlet. One or two found personal items that hadn't been burned or smashed and hauled them to the center of the ville where they were left.

As he watched, a few more men and women who had lived in the hamlet straggled from the tree line closest to Cambodia, moving toward him. All were dressed in black pajamas, and as they neared, it was evident they had spent the night and part of the day in hiding. There were mud stains on their clothes. Their faces and bodies were dirty. They followed the rice paddy dikes until they reached the high ground where the hamlet sat.

Two soldiers went out to meet the villagers, checking the first few for hidden weapons, and then escorting them in. Helmsman turned and glanced at the medic, but he was busy with the wounded found in the bunker.

Warren approached and said, "We'd better whistle up the choppers, sir, so we can get out of here soon."

"What's the rush? There's plenty of daylight left."

"Yes, sir, plenty. Except Charlie knows that if he hits us late in the afternoon, then there's a good chance we won't pursue him. The later the choppers show up, the better it is for him."

Helmsman shook his head. "Contact late in the day means that we bug out, that right?"

"Too hard to keep the men in the grass at night. Charlie gets a few cheap casualties that way."

"Okay," said Helmsman. He turned in a circle slowly, studying the scene around him. This had not been a normal hamlet. Instead of mud and thatch hootches, many of the structures had been made from plywood and brick. The dispensary and the school had been made of cinder blocks, but most of those were now broken. Both buildings looked like the rubble left after the carpenter and bricklayers were finished. The tin used on their roofs, and on the hootches were now twisted scraps of metal. The Vietcong had known what they were doing. They had left no structure intact, and had tried to destroy the materials to prevent rebuilding.

The RTO was crouching in the little area of shade created by a wall that hadn't collapsed. He held his canteen in one hand, drinking from it. His Adam's apple bobbed as he swallowed the warm water. When he finished, he poured a little on his go-to-hell rag and wiped at the back of his neck.

Helmsman moved toward him and took the handset from him. "What freq you on?"

"Company," said the man without looking up.

Helmsman squeezed the handset and made his call, requesting that the choppers be sent. They'd need one for evacuation of wounded. Not Americans but local indigenous personnel, none of them seriously hurt.

The reply wasn't what he expected. "Wait one."

"Roger."

He stood up and leaned against the wall. A moment later there was the call. "Black Raider one six, this is Black Raider three."

"Go three."

"Medevac chopper is inbound, your location. Be advised you are to remain on station now. Do you need resupply?"

Helmsman thought about the original mission and how the men hadn't bothered to carry much in the way of food. Plenty of water and ammunition, but no food. They had expected a hot meal in camp that night.

"Roger. We will need resupply."

"Choppers will be arranged for the resupply mission. You are to remain in place tonight. Orders to follow."

"Roger," said Helmsman. He waited and when there was nothing more from his operations officer, he flipped the handset to the RTO. He approached Warren, who was standing with two other men watching the Vietnamese.

"We're here for the night," Helmsman told them.

"Wait a minute, sir," said Warren.

"No, I know what you're going to say and it's all been taken care of. Medevac is coming in to take out the people the doc thinks will have to go, and we're getting resupply."

"What's going on?" asked Warren.

"Damned if I know," said Helmsman. "All I know is that **our orders have been changed.**"

"Well, shit!" said Warren. "We'd better scope this out and figure out some kind of defensive perimeter."

"At least we're not going to be in the jungle," said Helmsman, but he wasn't sure that not being in the jungle was a plus.

MORROW STOOD under the tower of the small terminal at Hotel Three, her camera bag at her feet. She was experiencing a slight feeling of discomfort. It wasn't the heat and humidity of the tropical afternoon, she knew, but the eyes of all the men waiting for rides back to their units. She didn't know if she should move outside, find a seat in the corner or stay where she was.

She was aware that the real problem was that the men hadn't seen many American women in the past few weeks or months. When there had been women to see they had been South Vietnamese. Now the men were standing next to her, wondering what they should do.

She tried to ignore them, watching the helicopters as they buzzed around the airfield. She concentrated on the aircraft hovering and landing or taking off, helicopters with M-60s mounted in the doors with men seated behind them. One of the choppers, a large yellow insect painted on the front, landed facing her. It seemed to squat there, waiting for a chance to leap into the sky.

"That's your ride now, Miss Morrow," yelled the sergeant behind the counter.

She picked up her camera bag and waved at the man, "Thanks." She hurried from the terminal and trotted toward the waiting helicopter. As she neared it, she ducked instinctively although the rotor blades were too high to pose any threat. Before she reached the chopper, the crew chief leaped to the ground, running toward her, one hand outstretched. He seized her camera bag and then helped her into the cargo compartment.

As she strapped herself in, the chopper picked up to a hover and spun. It hesitated for a moment and then lifted off, climbing out to the south. To the right she could see Tan Son Nhut Airport with its two long, narrow runways. They were bordered by sandbagged revetments for fighters and a hangar that she knew belonged to the CIA. The Air America pad was the worst-kept secret of the war. A silver and blue C-47 sat there while three or four men worked on it.

Just as they seemed to reach altitude, the cold air seeping into the chopper raising goose bumps, they began descending again, to race along the ground. Morrow had taken dozens of helicopter rides during her stay in Vietnam and this was the one thing she hated. Speeding along the ground, no more than two or three feet high, dodging and popping over obstacles. She grabbed the edge of the troop seat, her hands cramping and aching from the strain of holding on. She wanted to close her eyes, but they were glued to the windshield.

She saw trees coming at them, palms and coconuts in a solid mass looking like a green wall. She knew that they were going to crash and burn. But at the last moment the pilot jerked in an armload of pitch and they popped over the trees before dropping back toward the ground. She felt herself become weightless, straining at the seat belt, and then she was forced down in the seat as they turned. Out of the cargo compartment door she saw the ground rushing by and again thought she was about to die.

And then they began a rapid climb and she relaxed, even though she could feel her heart hammering in her chest and her hands shaking.

The crew chief looked around from the well where he sat, grinning. "You okay?" He had to shout to be heard over the sound of the turbine engine and the popping of the rotors.

Morrow didn't want to speak. She nodded once and tried not to think about the wild ride. If someone could figure out a way to get people to pay for such a ride, he'd get rich.

They continued to the west and the north. On one side of the chopper were wide stretches of swamp. Sunlight reflected from water. Clumps of trees were scattered throughout, but no hootches. On the other side was a tangled mess of short trees and thick brush known as the Hobo Woods. Farther on that changed to a rubber plantation that looked like a formation of tall, green troops marching to war. The Saigon River wound its way through the area.

Finally she saw Nui Ba Den in the distance. The Black Virgin Mountain dominated the countryside near the large Vietnamese city of Tay Ninh. American Special Forces held the top and the American Army controlled the bottom, but the interior and the sides belong to Charlie. She'd heard talk that there would someday be an operation to clear the enemy, but no one wanted to tackle the job.

The chopper entered the traffic pattern at Tay Ninh and headed toward the south. It hovered down the runway and then turned into the company area of the Crusaders. They landed on the perforated-steel-plate pad and the pilot turned, looking over the back of his armored seat.

"Hope the low leveling didn't bother you too much."

Morrow unbuckled her seat belt and shoved her camera bag toward the door. She crouched on the hard metal deck so that she was close to the pilot. Over the noise of the engine, she shouted, "Why do you do that?"

"Traffic at Tan Son Nhut. We have to low-level under the active runway, otherwise we snarl the traffic." He grinned broadly and added, "Besides, it's a hell of a ride. That's when you know you're flying."

Now she smiled back and agreed. "It *is* a hell of a ride." She moved to the door and dropped to the ground. As she walked across the pad toward the operations bunker, the chopper picked up to a hover. She felt the rotor wash tear at her back and watched the swirling cloud of dust as it engulfed her. She closed her eyes and stopped moving until the cloud had dissipated and the sound of the chopper was fading.

She walked into the operations bunker. It was made from the rubberized green sandbags that were becoming standard in Vietnam. Inside the door was a small entryway and another door to the left. A mortar or rocket exploding outside could put shrapnel into the entryway but not into the bunker proper. It served the same purpose as the Z entrance.

Inside the second door was another small room. This was a counter-and-window affair that reminded her of bus or train ticket offices. On one wall was a scheduling board listing who was flying which aircraft. There were no names on the board that she recognized.

"Can I help you?"

She turned and saw a young man standing behind the counter. He had light hair and the beginnings of a mustache and didn't look old enough to drive.

"Your mother know you're here?" she asked.

"Nope. That mean I can go home?"

"Afraid not. I need to catch a ride out to Duc Bang, small hamlet out near—"

"I know where it is," he said. "We've a resupply chopper going out there in about fifteen minutes. You can catch a ride on it. Providing, of course, you've got the proper authorization."

"No one ever asks for authorization. You pissed because of that crack about your mother."

"No, ma'am. It's just that we're supposed to get an authorization for every civilian."

"My press card do anything for you?"

"No, ma'am, it sure doesn't." He shook his head. "The press hasn't been real cooperative with the Army lately, with all those stories about how good the VC are and how ragtag we are."

Morrow set her bag on the concrete floor of the bunker. She crouched and opened one of the zippered pockets. She pulled a dirty, tattered paper from it and handed it to the operations clerk. "That do it for you?"

"Little worse for wear, but then most everything is." He glanced at it. "That does it. Chopper will take off from the VIP pad in about ten minutes. You can wait here. The AC'll be in and you can walk out with him."

"Thank you."

The clerk disappeared. Morrow stood there and then walked over to the scheduling board that hung in the corner near a naked light bulb. She noticed they seemed to be logging a great deal of flying time and it seemed they were going through aircraft fast. The numbers that had been lovingly printed on the board in black paint were scratched through and replaced in grease pencil. She also noticed that all the pilots' names were written in grease pencil. They didn't survive long enough to have someone paint their names on the board.

A man carrying a flight helmet stuck his head in the bunker. "You our pax?"

Morrow turned and saw a man who looked as young as the operations clerk. He wore jungle fatigues, a chest protector and an Old West-type holster on the left so that the butt faced her. He'd have to reach across his body to draw his weapon.

"If you're going out to Duc Bang."

He entered the bunker and asked, "What in the hell you want to go out there for?"

She picked up her camera bag. "Because that's where the story is."

"Well, come on and I'll see that you get out there." He held the door for her and then escorted her across dirt and peta-prime road to where his helicopter stood.

Before he climbed into the seat he asked, "You sure you want to do this?"

"You asking me that because I'm a woman?"

"No, ma'am," he said. "I'm asking you because it seems to be such a damn stupid thing to do."

GERBER SAT in the passenger seat of the jeep, a foot on the dash, staring straight ahead. "Well, that fucking tears it," he said.

Fetterman sat behind the wheel, but hadn't bothered to start the engine. "What do we do first?"

"I don't know. Where in the hell are we supposed to get an A-detachment? You can't just go to supply and draw one."

Fetterman rubbed his chin. "Maybe we can make a few calls and gather most of the team we had here on our first tour."

"Johnny's got a lot of them out at his camp near Song Be," said Gerber.

"You mean Jack?"

Gerber laughed. "Right, Jack." He'd forgotten that Bromhead, the exec on his first tour, had given up the name Johnny when he was promoted to captain.

"Seems to me," said Fetterman, "we could get Tyme and Bocker from him for a few weeks. Kepler's around again for Intel. Washington must be back by now if we can locate him. Add in Sully Smith for demolitions, and we've got a hell of a core to work with."

"Yeah," said Gerber, nodding. "We can hit Moc Hoa and pull in a company from the Mike Force there until we can get things organized. That might be the thing to do."

"Then our only real problem is persuading Bromhead to let us borrow his people and track down the others."

"And to finish it off," said Gerber, "we could ask MACV-SOG for a few people. Get General Padgett to make a phone call or two. Take a day or so to organize."

Now Fetterman grinned. "And give you another night in Saigon with Miss Morrow."

"Well, I hadn't really thought about that, but yes, it would give me another night in Saigon."

Fetterman reached up to the dash and turned the ignition switch. He backed out slowly, the gravel crunching under the tires of the jeep. He left the parking lot and turned onto the street. "Where are we going?"

"I haven't thought about that. Let's head on over to Tan Son Nhut."

"Any reason for that?" asked Fetterman.

"Well, the new MACV-SOG staging area is there and we can find out who's around with nothing to do."

Fetterman pulled to the side of the road, judged the traffic and then turned around. He put his foot on the gas, speeding up until they entered the flow of traffic. Almost immediately, they were surrounded by bicycles, motorbikes, Hondas and all the other military vehicles. They skirted the edge of the city, staying on the northern perimeter until they came to the front gate at Tan Son Nhut. Now the MPs stopped everyone who wanted to enter, checked the ID cards and papers of all the South Vietnamese, turning the majority of them away.

"That's got to piss off the troops," said Gerber.

"How so?"

"Because the majority of the people who are turned back are the prostitutes. They're really not much of a threat to the base's security, but the military mind has declared them all to be nonessential personnel. The ones they should keep out, the maintenance workers, the shit burners and the like, are allowed on the base, and if anyone is Vietcong it'll be those people.''

When they reached the gate, the guard waved them through without stopping them. It was obvious that they were American soldiers.

Inside the compound, they drove slowly along the narrow roads. There were barracks, two-story structures that the military had been building since before World War II. Many of them had sandbags around the bottom floor. Others were lined by fifty-five-gallon drums that were filled with sand. The base was crawling with men and women, circulating among the various offices, maintenance sheds, clubs and BXs.

They turned and came to a single-story building. Fetterman parked in front of it and looped the chain bolted to the jeep's floor through the steering wheel. It was the only way they had of locking the vehicle to prevent theft. The thief would probably be a ''supply'' officer for another unit who had a need for the jeep. It was a constant game in the military. Replace your stolen or missing property by stealing it from someone else.

Before they got out, Fetterman asked, ''How are you going to handle this?''

''Hadn't thought much about it. Probably see who's around and let them know what we need. If we don't get some volunteers, then I'll try to dragoon a couple.''

Fetterman got out and walked to the door, with Gerber right behind him. Fetterman opened the door and the captain entered. To the right was a dayroom, paneled with plywood that had been darkened with a blow torch to bring out the grain. A small air conditioner was built into the wall, and although it didn't turn the place into the arctic waste favored by the generals at MACV, the air was cooler than outside.

The humidity had been wrung from the air so that it was comfortable inside the building.

Gerber entered the dayroom, which had been decorated with captured weapons: AKs, SKSs, RPDs and RPGs. Photographs of men in jungle fatigues, grinning at the cameras, hung on the walls. There was also a huge poster of Ann-Margret that had been signed by her. To one side a table was stacked with magazines, paperbacks and newspapers. Almost all of them dealt with sex. In one corner sat a beat-up couch with one leg missing. It had been replaced with a brick. There were chairs, a refrigerator that rocked back and forth, a small black-and-white TV and not a single person.

"This looks bad," said Fetterman.

"Yeah, I'd hoped to find a few guys in here."

"Looks like everyone's out."

Gerber shrugged and they walked through the building. They found just four men working in the back. All had been given assignments and were working on their equipment before deploying into the field. They weren't interested in anything Gerber had going.

"Where is everyone?" asked Gerber.

One of the men looked up. "In the field. And I mean everyone. Since Tet, we've been busy."

Gerber looked at the sergeant. "I heard that."

"So now what are we going to do?" asked Fetterman.

"Guess we should have talked to Jerry Maxwell before coming over here, or gone to tell Padgett what we'd need so that it could be arranged. If that fails, then I guess we'll have to punt."

"I don't think this is going to be as easy as we thought."

"I'm afraid you're right on that."

4

IN THE AIR, SOUTH OF
DUC BANG, REPUBLIC
OF VIETNAM

Unlike the last flight Robin had taken, this one was relatively sane. The pilot had climbed to fifteen hundred feet and stayed there. He had not come close to any other aircraft, had not dived out of the sun in imitation of World War II fighter planes and had not insisted on low-leveling. Although it was cool at altitude, Morrow found it relaxing. It was good to get away from the oppressive heat and humidity of the ground.

For a moment she relaxed, enjoying herself. She studied the landscape passing underneath them. Dark greens and tans and reds. Clumps of tall trees that protected the hootches of rice farmers. Small villages that were little more than a collection of hootches made of mud and thatch, a few with tin roofs that rusted in the humid tropical environment. People were working in the rice fields—men and women in black wearing coolie hats and refusing to look up at the helicopter, men walking behind water buffalo as they plowed their fields, kids running from one another, some of them naked because it was too hot for clothes.

Morrow took a camera from her bag, changed lenses and snapped a few photographs, trying to capture the essence of the country. She unfastened her seat belt, crouched in the doorway of the cargo compartment to take a few more and then slid to the right to change the angles. Below her were people who didn't care about the war, except when it was raging around them. They were too busy trying to eke out a miserable existence to worry about the war. They were too busy trying to stay alive.

The crew chief looked around from his well and shouted, "We're about five minutes out." He pointed with a gloved hand. "You can just make it out in the distance."

Morrow turned and stared through the windshield. There seemed to be an unbroken sea of green. Then there was a gigantic clearing, a light green that contrasted with the dark of the surrounding jungle. The hamlet sat on one side. There was another village, a mile or two away, nestled in the same clearing.

Morrow took a picture through the front of the helicopter, the pilot's head and shoulder bracketing it on one side. As they got closer, she took more pictures. At first she could tell nothing about the hamlet, other than it was there, a gray-black smudge against the tropical green. But as they flew closer, she could see that something was wrong. Instead of looking like the model village that Saigon had claimed it to be, it looked like a mouth full of broken teeth.

Morrow settled back onto the troop seat. They circled the hamlet once and she shot more pictures through the cargo compartment door. On one side of the village, a cloud of green began to billow, and Morrow photographed the men as they scurried around, preparing for the helicopter's landing.

The pilot began the descent, slipping closer to the ground, aiming at the cloud of green smoke drifting on the perimeter of the hamlet. For a moment Morrow was afraid of an enemy ambush, but then realized that the men were standing around waiting. If there were enemy in the area, they wouldn't be standing up, watching the chopper come in.

The helicopter flared and Morrow lost sight of them and the hamlet. Then the chopper settled to the ground, the green smoke sucked in by the rotor wash. As the skids hit the ground, both the door gunner and the crew chief were out, pitching the boxes of C-rations onto the ground. Two of the grunts came over and helped. When they finished, Morrow grabbed her camera bag and leaped out.

"Ain't you goin' back with us?" shouted the door gunner over the popping of the rotors.

"I'll stay here for a while," she shouted back.

The man moved closer and said, "AC thinks you should go back with us."

Morrow shook her head and glanced at the chopper. Both pilots were looking at her. "You tell them I'll be fine. I need to get some pictures down here."

"Okay." He turned and climbed back into the rear of the chopper. He sat behind one of the M-60 machine guns, plugged the cord from his flight helmet into the intercom system and held a thumb up.

Morrow retreated a couple of steps as the chopper got light on the skids. It lifted, hovering a few feet off the ground, creating a windstorm that seized anything that was lying loose, flipping it into the air. The engine roar drowned out all other sound.

The aircraft then leaped into the sky, climbing toward the south. In moments it was quiet. The grunts stood staring at Morrow, surprised to see her there. Finally one of them came forward.

"Excuse me," said the man, "but what in the hell are you doing here?"

She held out a hand. "I'm here to do a story. Find out what happened, interview the people and some of your men. You are...?"

"Lieutenant Kenneth Helmsman. This is my platoon sergeant, Paul Warren."

"Hello," said Morrow.

"Excuse me," said Helmsman, "but this isn't a secured area. We made contact with the VC as we came in. You really shouldn't be here."

"I plan to take the next chopper out," Morrow said. "But in the meantime I have a story to do and I'd like to talk to some of the villagers."

"You speak Vietnamese?" asked Warren.

"No. I figured someone with your party could interpret."

"I'm afraid not," said Helmsman. "We're a line unit, sent out to look at what happened here. Sergeant Warren has a smattering of the language but not much. By the way, there's no other chopper coming in tonight."

Morrow shouldered her bag. "That's fine by me. Give me more of a chance to learn what's going on."

"We're not set up to take care of a woman," protested Helmsman. "No one told us you were coming."

"You don't have to take care of me. I can take care of myself. Just give me a little water and a C-ration meal, and I'll be happy."

Helmsman looked at Warren and said, "Assign Corporal Russell to her."

"That'll make him very happy.

"Tell him not to get too happy. I'll have my eye on him." He turned his attention back to Morrow but didn't speak right away. He was trying to decide what to say to her. Finally he settled on, "Glad to have you with us." He didn't sound as if he meant it.

As Helmsman walked away from the woman he wondered whom she'd talked to in order to get herself into the field unescorted. It was rare enough to see a reporter and almost an impossibility to see a woman. If something happened to her, it would be front page news all over the world, and she was one problem he didn't need. Not with the enemy somewhere in the area.

He found a corporal and asked, "What we got out for security?"

"Squad spread around the perimeter watching the trees, with orders to stay put until relieved. Rest of the platoon is still searching."

Helmsman nodded, realizing he should have known that without asking. This wasn't the ROTC, where he wasn't supposed to know everything. This was combat in Vietnam, where the men were looking to him for the answers.

He stood and looked at the hamlet. A couple of his men were crouched near the remains of a bunker, watching the open ground in front of them. Others were still poking into the hootches, while four or five stood near the Vietnamese villagers.

Helmsman was suddenly angry. He didn't like this change in the mission. There were too many things that could go wrong too easily. The men hadn't been prepared for a night in the field. Mentally, they'd been ready for the choppers to take them back to the base camp. They wouldn't be alert during the night. They would dope off because they had expected to be at the camp that night.

He turned and saw that Warren had introduced Morrow to Corporal Russell, a wiry youngster who had dropped out of high school to join the Army. Russell was one of the youngest men in the platoon but had been in Vietnam for six months. He was shy yet tough. If anyone could take good care of the reporter, he could, without embarrassing the Army.

Helmsman walked over to where the Vietnamese crouched and the medic still worked. "You get everyone evaced you want to?" he asked.

"Yes, sir. That was no problem."

Helmsman studied the Vietnamese. No one had moved since they were herded out of the bunker. It was getting late in the day, and that meant none of them had eaten since the night before.

"Let's get these people out of the open. Break out one of the cases of C-rations and see that everyone gets something to eat. Make sure there are enough meals left for our platoon and the reporter. The Vietnamese can share a meal if they have to."

"Yes, sir."

Helmsman turned again and felt the anger bubbling through him. He was stuck in the field with a female reporter and a bunch of Vietnamese. He wanted to be back at his camp, sucking down beer and maybe watching a movie. He wanted to punch something or someone. It was too hot and miserable to be in the field. His head ached and he was thirsty, but the water tasted of plastic and halozone.

Then he realized that being angry would do no good. He'd just have to begin to think his way through the problem. One squad on alert throughout the night while the other two slept, rotating so that everyone got a good rest. Someone would have to keep an eye on the Vietnamese, just in case. RTO should set up in the remains of the arms locker because it was centrally located and had good protection.

With the hootches and bunkers, there would be shelter for everyone in case it rained. He conceded that it wasn't as comfortable as it would have been at the camp and there would be no movie, but it wasn't as bad as it could have been. At least they weren't in the jungle.

Warren joined him. "How do you want to handle this?"

Helmsman explained the plan and Warren nodded. "Good idea. We can also coordinate with the arty advisory so they're on call if we need illumination or artillery support."

The Vietnamese began to move as the Americans handed out the C-ration meals. They scattered, moving to the hootches that they had occupied. No one seemed inclined to dig through the rubble and no one approached the pile of personal items stacked in the hamlet square.

"This is going to be one long, miserable night," said Helmsman, the anger back.

"Not too bad," said Warren philosophically. "At least no one is shooting at us."

"Yet," added Helmsman.

ON THEIR RETURN to MACV Headquarters, Gerber and Fetterman walked up to the office that belonged to General Padgett. It was in a corner at the end of a long hallway. The dark wood of the mahogany door was in stark contrast to everything else, which was painted green.

Fetterman raised an eyebrow when he saw it, but Gerber didn't hesitate. He opened it and stepped in. There was a single large desk in the center of the office and a Vietnamese woman sat behind it. Long, black hair, an oval face, dark eyes and small nose. She was wearing an *ao dai*.

"You want?" she asked when she saw them.

"General Padgett. Is he in?"

She stood, bowed slightly and asked, "Who calling?"

"Captain Gerber and Sergeant Fetterman."

"You wait and I see if general is in?"

When she disappeared, Fetterman whispered, "You think she's more than a secretary?"

"Sergeant Fetterman, are you suggesting that a general officer would hire this woman for something other than her secretarial talents?"

"Yes, sir."

"Well, you're probably right. Everyone else has a male clerk, though she seems to be doing a good job."

"I guess only the general would know that," retorted Fetterman with a straight face.

She returned, bowing. "General will see you now. Please to follow."

They entered Padgett's office. Gerber was surprised. It wasn't the luxurious surroundings that he had expected. The desk, though made of dark wood, was smaller than the one outside. There was no fancy paneling, just walls painted the same green as most of the other offices in the building. There were blinds on the windows but no curtains. Three chairs, no couch and a single painting that had been purchased in downtown Saigon, created by a local artist.

Padgett stood as they entered. "I didn't expect to see the two of you again so soon. Please, sit down. Thank you, *co*."

When the woman was gone, Gerber came directly to the point. "We might need help creating the team. The problem is that Special Forces have been spread so thin since Tet, it's almost impossible to assemble a team in-country."

Padgett dropped into his chair and plucked a pipe from the rack sitting on his desk. He dipped it into the humidor, tamped it down and then lighted it. He puffed until there was a cloud of blue drifting around his head.

"You have a problem with using regular Army troops on this team of yours?"

"Meaning?"

"Simply that if you don't insist on a Special Forces trained radioman, I can get you one quickly. That sort of thing. Regular Army provides good training for the specials."

"If we can get a commo man from Special Forces to work over him, set up a team and fill in the junior slots with specialists. That would work."

"You give me a list of who you want and I'll have them at Hotel Three at seven tomorrow morning waiting for you."

"General," said Gerber, "I can get you a list of people I'd like to see, but we have to be careful. A couple of men are at Song Be, assigned to the team there. I don't want to strip that camp to make up my team. I don't want to put any team into a bind to satisfy the requirements of this mission."

It was silent in the office for a moment with only the hum of the air conditioner disturbing the quiet. The general puffed on his pipe and stared at the ceiling as if lost in thought.

"I would think," said the general, "that I'm clever enough not to strip a camp."

"Yes, sir," said Gerber. "We'd also like permission to take a company of strikers from the Mike Force at Moc Hoa, preferring Nung if we can get them."

"Any special reason for that?"

"Nung wouldn't be infiltrated by the Vietcong. Those tribesmen hate the Vietnamese with such a passion that none of them would be Communist or Vietcong."

"I see," the general said. "Anything else?"

"Just one question," said Gerber. "We'd like to know why this hamlet has become so important."

"I think," said Padgett, "that it's enough to know that someone thinks it's important. Besides, you heard the reasons at the briefing this afternoon."

"In the Special Forces, we normally have a few better answers than that," Gerber said.

Padgett took his pipe from between his teeth and set it in the ashtray. He stared at Gerber for a moment, then shifted his gaze to Fetterman. "Normally, as a general officer, I'm not questioned like this. I give an order and people go out to obey it."

"Yes, General," said Gerber, waiting.

"But we're all professionals here. Let me just say that we want to prove to the Vietcong that we'll not be pushed out of an area. We'll hold on to it if we feel it's important. This hamlet has been deemed important. It's to become an object lesson for the enemy."

"Fair enough," said Gerber.

"Now, I expect you people at Hotel Three in the morning, ready for duty in the field. I'll arrange transport, or have it arranged. There's a platoon of Americans out there tonight, and you'll be authorized to hold them on site if you feel you need them. At least for a couple of days. Construction supplies, ammo, food and anything else will be yours for the asking."

"Yes, sir," said Gerber.

"Now, if there's nothing else . . ."

Gerber got to his feet. "The list of men we'd like."

Fetterman handed over a sheet of paper. "I took the liberty of making the list while you two were talking. The first name in each slot is the man we'd like, the second is an alternate if the first is not available."

"You want to see it?" Padgett looked at Gerber.

"No, sir. If Sergeant Fetterman prepared it, it will be perfect."

"Then I'll get on it," said Padgett. He picked up his pipe again.

Gerber stood for a moment and then headed out the door, Fetterman right behind him.

In the outer office, Fetterman asked, "What now?"

"You have everything you need ready to go?"

"You know I do," said Fetterman. "Just as everyone else in Special Forces does."

"Then rather than going back to work, we can go eat dinner."

"That mean you're hungry or are you looking for an excuse to call Miss Morrow?"

"It means that I'm looking for an excuse to call Miss Morrow," said Gerber.

"Then by all means, let's hurry on downtown so that you can get something to eat."

5

THE HAMLET OF DUC BANG, REPUBLIC OF VIETNAM

After the Americans had handed out the C-rations, the Vietnamese seemed to relax. Morrow had noticed the surprise register on their faces, then noticed that the fear seemed to evaporate. It was as if they had expected the Americans to kill them, but now that the soldiers were giving them food, they knew they would live a while longer.

She moved toward a group of them and sat down near them to eat her dinner. Opening the cardboard box, she sorted through the cans, looking to see what she'd gotten. She used one of the tiny P-38s to open the can, set it on the ground and opened the plastic-wrapped spoon. Putting that in her pocket, she opened a packet of salt and sprinkled it on the boned chicken. Finished, she looked up, saw that two people were watching her. She smiled at them, bowing slightly.

They watched her eat and then began to open the cans that had been given them. Both sat down so they could keep an eye on Morrow. When they were comfortable, she moved slightly closer.

"Good food," she said, not because the food was good, but because it was something to say. She kept her voice low.

Neither of the Vietnamese responded to her comment. They opened their cans, one of ham and lima beans and the other of scrambled eggs. They didn't bother with the plastic spoon, but scooped the food out with their fingers, pushing it into their mouths.

Again Morrow shifted closer. She noticed that the woman was in her mid-thirties, maybe older, and from the slight bulge of her stomach, possibly pregnant. The male was considerably younger. He wore only black shorts and didn't seem to have the upper body development that hinted at a Vietcong soldier. His shoulders and chest weren't heavily muscled.

"Do you speak English?" Morrow asked.

The boy stared at her and shook his head. It meant that he did understand a few phrases, but probably didn't have a command of the language.

Morrow took a big bite and then put down the can. She wished she had peaches or pears, but the fruit wasn't packed into many of the meals. She figured the soldiers had gotten all the fruit.

"What happened here?" she asked, her eyes flitting from one person to the other. Neither spoke to her.

Russell loomed out of the growing dusk and fell to the ground next to her. He slung his rifle and tried not to stare at her bare legs. He opened his meal and said, "Zips don't talk much."

"They're people, not zips," she said automatically.

"Yes, ma'am. Sorry. They just don't talk much. Don't speak much English. At least that's what they claim."

Morrow wanted to reach for her notebook, but didn't. She asked, "Why do you say that?"

"Come on. They're living in a hamlet built by us, eating food brought by us and being protected by us. They must have learned some English."

"The protection wasn't all that great last night," Morrow reminded him.

"Yes, ma'am, but only because our people were ordered out. Marvin ARVN didn't have to go, he just did. There were weapons left behind."

"I'm aware of the results of that. Fifteen, twenty of the men dead."

Russell fell silent. Morrow looked at the two Vietnamese, but they had moved away from her. Their eyes were on the soldier with the M-16 slung over his shoulder. It was as if they were waiting for the other shoe to fall.

"Why are these people afraid of you?" she asked.

"I don't know," said Russell. "Weird, isn't it? You'd think they'd be happy to see us."

"Maybe the Vietcong told them that if the Americans came back they'd all be killed."

Russell shook his head. "Doesn't seem likely. If that was the case, why wouldn't they all have taken off?"

That was the question that Morrow could never answer. In Nazi Germany, with the government pouring out hate for the Jews every minute of the day, arresting hundreds in the dead of night, why had so many stayed? When war threatened France, why didn't the people get out? The only answer was that people didn't want to leave their homes. They were trapped by their birthright and their material possessions, no matter how meager those possessions were.

"There's more here than meets the eye," Morrow said.

"Why are you so interested in these people, anyway?"

Morrow looked at him closely. "Aren't you?"

"No, ma'am. I'm interested in getting through this tour and getting the hell out. I don't care about the Vietnamese.

They're all thieves and con artists and prostitutes. They'll steal you blind, and we're supposed to accept it because that's the way they are. And if they're not stealing from you, they're setting you up for the VC or the NVA."

The Vietnamese youth shook his head violently and said, "No VC. No VC."

Russell grinned. "Sure. I know that." He turned toward Morrow. "Little punk is probably the enemy's number-one agent."

Again the boy recognized a word. "GI numbah one. VC numbah ten."

"Christ," said Russell.

"Don't you understand that these people are frightened?"

"And don't you understand that I don't give a shit? If they had any guts at all, they'd be fighting their own damned war and I wouldn't have to be here getting my butt shot off. Where in the hell is their own army anyway? Every time there's shooting, the ARVN are gone in a cloud of dust."

"They've done their share of the fighting."

"Oh, you think so," demanded Russell. He lowered his voice and looked around as if afraid someone would overhear him. "Let me tell you something. If an American unit hits light contact, they'll be reinforced with ARVN. Let the little bastards get a taste of fighting without real danger. If it's heavy contact, then the reinforcements will be more Americans. And if the ARVN stumble into contact, they're always reinforced by Americans. What's that tell you?"

"Tells me that maybe you shouldn't be here." She was thinking of Gerber's attitude toward the South Vietnamese and how it differed from Russell's. She'd never heard Gerber express such doubts about the capabilities of the South Vietnamese.

Russell snorted his response. "Maybe I shouldn't be here. What fucking choice did I have? Government says you're going to be drafted and if you don't comply with the law, you're going to jail. I'll write my congressman and tell him you think I shouldn't be here."

"Sorry," Morrow said. "I wasn't thinking about that. I just thought maybe we ought to think about how the South Vietnamese feel about this."

"Who the fuck cares?" said Russell again, his voice rising. Then he realized that he was nearly shouting and he'd been ordered to stay close to the lady reporter. "Sorry."

Morrow didn't speak for a moment. She was thinking about the different attitude of the professional soldier, who looked at the war as something more than the clash of two opposing armies. He looked at the overall picture of what a defeat would mean, not only to the men in uniform but to the people of the region. Morrow wasn't sure she subscribed to the theory that a Communist victory would lead to a massive bloodbath, though that seemed a real possibility. Thousands had been murdered in Hue when the Communists took the city. That might be a preview of things to come.

Gerber, and men like him, were concerned about the people who might be caught in the cross fire. They thought about the consequences of their actions. But at the other end of the spectrum were the draftees, who had two years to spend in the Army and if they were lucky, they'd never get to Vietnam. If they did, they viewed the war as something to survive. When the people didn't seem to welcome them, when they stole from them and aided the enemy, the draftees saw it as a danger to their lives. They learned not to trust the Vietnamese and came to hate them all.

Morrow realized that she could understand their attitude. She'd seen enough of the war to understand it. She'd seen the body of the local tailor, hanging in the wire of the base camp after he led a VC attack. She knew of a prostitute who tried to cut the throats of the Americans she serviced.

And when the friendliest of the Vietnamese turned out to be the enemy in disguise, the Americans learned that they couldn't tell the enemy from the friendlies. It was easier to hate everyone. In fact, it might be healthier.

"Sorry," said Russell again, breaking into her thoughts.

"It's okay," Morrow said, "I understand." She picked up her can and finished eating the boned chicken.

As the sun disappeared and the hamlet was wrapped in darkness, Helmsman approached Morrow. "I think you should take shelter in the arms locker."

"Why?"

Helmsman rubbed his chin. "This area isn't the most secure in the world. I think it would be better if we stayed under cover as much as possible tonight. Charlie has to know we're here. He couldn't have missed the choppers and he knows we didn't pull out. I don't want to give him any targets."

Morrow stood and brushed the dirt from her seat. She started to pick up the remains of her meal, but Helmsman told her to forget it. Someone else would do that.

"You in a big hurry?"

Before the lieutenant could answer, there was a distant pop, like a firecracker in a trash can.

Helmsman put a hand on her chest and pushed her to the ground. "Incoming!" he yelled as he dived to the dirt. His helmet popped off and he had to scramble to recover it.

There was a single detonation on the other side of the hamlet. For a moment it was quiet and Helmsman got to his feet. Then came a series of pops and he dived back to the ground, rolling toward Morrow as if to protect her.

The second explosion was closer. Shrapnel slashed through the air, and dirt rained down. Morrow could smell the dust and the cordite and her ears were ringing. But the third round landed farther away and the rest hit near the perimeter.

As the last one exploded, Helmsman was on his feet again. He crouched near the corner of the concrete arms locker and shouted, "Anyone got the tubes spotted?"

The only answer was a rippling of small-arms fire, M-16s and M-60s opening up. The ruby-red tracers flashed across the open paddies and into the tree line a couple of hundred yards away.

Helmsman spun and stuck his face close to Morrow. "You hurt?"

"No." She crawled to the left until she was at the base of the concrete wall. She stuck her face into it, breathing in the dirt.

Helmsman was moving then, running across the open ground toward the perimeter. He leaped over a pile of rubble, stumbled and fell to his knees. To the right he saw the RTO, lying facedown. Helmsman ran to him and shouted at him. "You hurt?"

"No, sir."

"Get the arty advisory on the radio. Let's see if we can do some damage."

As he took the handset from the RTO, he realized that all the firing was outgoing. One machine gun and a half dozen M-16s. He dropped the handset and ordered, "Cease firing. Cease firing."

Warren appeared out of the darkness. "Nothing on the other sides of the hamlet. Just the one group in the trees to the south. Think we should go after them?"

"Our orders are to stay here," Helmsman said.

"But we know where the enemy is."

"That's right, Sergeant," said Helmsman. He knew he was doing the right thing. "But we were not ordered to engage the enemy. We're to hold this ground. Besides, we don't know the size of the enemy force and could be walking into an ambush. Probably would be."

"Yes, sir," said Warren. "I'll advise the men to stay put."

"And tell them not to fire unless they have a target. We don't have to advertise the location of our emplacements."

"Yes, sir."

Helmsman got to his feet and, ducking low, ran toward the center of the hamlet. He found Morrow sitting with her back to the wall of the arms locker, her elbows on her knees and her head in her hands, staring into the night.

"You don't seem too concerned about this," he said as he dropped to the ground beside her.

"I've been through mortar attacks before. If they're not coming at you, there isn't much to worry about."

"That was just a harassment raid to see if they could draw us out. I don't have the men to make grandstand plays."

"Lieutenant, what in the hell are you doing here?"

He turned to look at her. He could just make out her face and shape in the light from the moon and the stars. There was a single fire burning near the perimeter, but no one seemed inclined to put it out.

"What do you mean?" he asked.

"Just that you don't seem like you belong here."

He shrugged. "I belong as much as any of us. I could ask you the same question."

"Yes, you could," she said. And I wouldn't have a good answer, she added mentally. She thought of Gerber and then her job, and couldn't figure out which one kept her in Vietnam. There were other beats to cover, but none with the high profile of Vietnam. And none of them had Gerber, either. Which was more important to her?

And then she answered herself because she knew what it was. She rarely let herself answer the question, sometimes picking at it like a scab. It was Gerber, pure and simple. After he'd rotated to the World and taken up again with Robin's sister, she'd stayed in Vietnam because she couldn't face life without him. She'd buried herself in her work. But her sister had turned into a jerk and Gerber had dumped her. Now Morrow couldn't leave Vietnam because that was where Gerber was. Funny how the man could keep her in the stink hole no matter where he was.

She touched the thoughts gingerly and then pushed them away, telling herself that she was kidding herself. She was in Vietnam because it was the only story worth covering. When she finally returned stateside, she would be able to name her price and her position because the credentials would be there.

"So what's the plan of action now?" she asked.

"We hang loose, watch for the bad guys and wait for morning when our relief should arrive. Then it's home to a warm shower and hot food."

"You mind if I look around and talk to your men?"

"Not as long as you don't silhouette yourself and don't distract the men." He laughed. "Well, any more than you already have."

GERBER STOOD in the lobby of the Continental Hotel, watching the men and women circulate through it. It was a cavernous room filled with potted palms, chairs and couches, marble columns and a desk with a couple of clerks. And all kinds of people. Men in uniforms and in suits. Women in uniforms and in dresses. American men and women and Vietnamese men and women. The Vietnamese women looked like prostitutes in their incredibly short skirts and tight blouses, which was unfortunate because most of them weren't.

Gerber had changed into the only civilian clothes he had. Tan pants and a blue shirt. He stood waiting for Fetterman, who had gone to his room to shower and change. He was supposed to meet both Gerber and Morrow in the lobby.

When he appeared a moment later, he said, "Where's Miss Morrow?"

Gerber shrugged. "Apparently out on an assignment. Her boss wouldn't tell me a thing. Probably afraid I'd tell every other journalist in Saigon."

"Would you?"

Gerber laughed. "If it wasn't Robin's story, I probably would, just to piss him off."

"That does nothing for our relationship with the working press," counseled Fetterman.

"So what? The working press has turned into our biggest enemy in Vietnam."

"That include Miss Morrow?"

"Of course not." Gerber studied Fetterman for a moment and asked, "What's with the suit and tie?"

"We were going to dinner and I thought I should dress. I took the liberty of securing companionship for myself, too."

Although he knew the answer before he asked the question, he still said, "And who might that be?"

Fetterman pointed at the door where Brouchard Bien Soo Ta Emilie, known as Kit, was entering. Kit was a former Vietcong who worked for the Americans. She was tall for a Vietnamese and had a narrow face, unlike most Orientals. Her eyes had only a hint of a slant and were dark blue, nearly violet, inherited from her father, a French soldier. The long jet-black hair was from her mother. Unlike the other Vietnamese women, she was dressed conservatively. She wore a knee-length black skirt and a white blouse that buttoned to the throat.

"Kit," said Gerber, as she approached them.

"Mack," she said, bowing slightly. "Where is Miss Morrow?"

"Working, I'm afraid. She won't be joining us this evening."

Kit moved so that she stood between the two men. She took one arm from each of them. Gerber was aware of her breast pressing against his biceps. She grinned at him.

Gerber pulled away and said, "I feel like the fifth wheel. Why don't you two go out and have something to eat and I'll stay here."

Kit turned to face him and stepped close, no more than six inches from him. She looked up into his eyes and said, "That's not necessary. We don't mind you tagging along." She shot a glance over her shoulder. "You tell him, Tony. Make him come to dinner with us."

Fetterman was clearly enjoying the scene. He knew that Kit had the hots for Gerber. Any opportunity to be with him without Morrow was one that she wouldn't pass up.

"I think you should join us, Captain. Wouldn't be right to leave you behind."

"Not right at all," Kit echoed.

"Robin might finish and come back. I wouldn't want to miss her."

"She leave a message?" asked Fetterman.

Gerber glared at him. "No, but you know how it is with these journalists."

"Look, Captain," said Fetterman, "we're not getting anywhere standing here. Miss Morrow probably won't be back tonight, otherwise she'd be here now. You might as well come to dinner with us."

For an instant, Gerber was going to refuse. The safest course was to beat a hasty retreat. He knew that. But then, he didn't like the idea of sitting in a hotel room on what could be his last night in Saigon for quite a while. He didn't know how long he'd be in the field or what the conditions at the hamlet would be like. Fetterman was right. He should go to dinner with them.

"All right, Tony. Let's go get something to eat. What did you have in mind?"

Fetterman began moving toward the door. Kit grabbed Gerber's hand and dragged him after them. She managed to bump into him as frequently as possible.

"Just thought maybe we'd go over to the Carasel and eat on their rooftop, among the tropical plants and under the stars."

"You're kidding, of course." Gerber couldn't understand the fascination of picnics and eating outside—not after having to eat C-rations in the jungle.

"Well, if you don't like that, we could eat here. The restaurants have passable food."

"Makes no real difference," said Gerber.

They stopped at the doors that would lead them into the tropical night. There were hundreds of people on the street, walking from one club to another. The traffic had thinned but was still heavy.

"If it makes no difference," said Fetterman, "then I'll choose and you can follow along."

"That'll be fine," Gerber said. Kit was standing right next to him and he could feel pressure from her thigh, hip and shoulder. She held his hand, and had pressed her breast against him again.

"This is going to be fun," she said.

"Sure," said Gerber, but he felt like the Seventh Cavalry as they rode toward the Little Bighorn. *Fun* just wasn't the right word for it.

6

THE HAMLET OF DUC BANG, REPUBLIC OF VIETNAM

Morrow crouched in the darkness at the edge of the hamlet and stared toward the tree line where the mortars had been hidden. In the past hour, there had been no more firing and she suspected that the enemy was moving the tubes so they could shoot again from a different location.

She had taken out a camera and loaded with black-and-white film. She knew it could be pushed in the developing, enabling her to photograph things in relative darkness, but it was too dark even for that. At best she would only get shapes and shadows, and while that kind of picture could be effective and was sometimes considered art, she first needed some interesting shapes to photograph.

She turned and looked back into the hamlet. The only movement was from the American soldiers as they changed the guard, or as Helmsman and Warren checked the perimeter. Someone had a battery-powered radio playing somewhere. She heard quiet, discordant sounds of Vietnamese music broken by pops and bursts of static.

Morrow got to her feet and headed toward the arms locker. As she reached it, a single shot hit the cement near her, chipping it. A piece clipped her on the hand, and she jerked once and fell to the side. She held up her hand, trying to see it in the dark. It stung as if she had nicked herself with a razor. As she licked the blood from the cut, she realized that if she had been in the Army, she would have qualified for a Purple Heart.

Firing erupted on the perimeter, M-16s on full auto. Morrow got to her feet and then loped across the hamlet, throwing herself to the ground as she approached the perimeter. The outgoing tracers burned bright red, disappearing into the trees. A few hit something and then bounced high, tumbling upward.

Morrow crawled forward slowly, staying on her belly but keeping her head high, watching the show. The firing began to taper and another round was fired at them, a single green tracer that passed over everyone's head.

The M-60 machine gun opened up, stitching a line of tracers through the jungle in front of them. An M-79 popped, but the round was short. A flash of light and a fountain of sparks mushroomed fifty yards from the trees.

Helmsman appeared and dropped to the ground near her. "It's nothing. Just harassment."

"They're doing a good job of it. You think they're preparing for an assault?"

Helmsman looked at his watch, peeling the camouflaged cover from it so that he could see the glowing hands. "I doubt it. They'd hit us with a big mortar and rocket barrage first, and I think that would have started already."

"Except," Morrow countered, "they tip their hand too early and it gives you a chance to prepare."

Helmsman rolled to his stomach and lifted the binoculars to his eyes. He scanned the tree line, but nothing was moving in there. Tracer rounds struck the trees and another M-79 round exploded.

"These guys will use any excuse to fire their weapons. They're just like kids with a new toy."

"Why don't you order them not to shoot back?" asked Morrow.

"Because, in this situation, I'd rather have them slightly trigger-happy than afraid to shoot."

The firing began to taper off again. There were a couple of sporadic shots and then silence.

Morrow whispered, "Aren't you afraid you'll run out of ammo in case something happens?"

"That's the least of our problems." He lowered his binoculars. "Why are you still running around? I'd be asleep now, if I had the chance."

"Well, maybe I'm afraid I'll miss something. Besides, I've been in Saigon where I got all the sleep I needed."

Helmsman scanned the trees again and then put his binoculars into the case. He slipped back so that his head was below the level of the berm, and he glanced up at Morrow. "I really wish you'd stay near the arms locker. It's the safest place in the hamlet."

"Stop providing interesting shows and I'll stay put." She grinned. After moving a short distance away from the perimeter, she sat up and looked into the hamlet. There was a story here, she was sure, but she didn't know what it was. It just didn't seem to be the one that she'd been sent out to get.

"I'm going to make another circuit of the hamlet," said Helmsman "If you need anything, please holler."

"Don't worry about it." She got to her feet, kept her head down and returned to the safety of the arms locker.

PADGETT SAT in his office, the only light coming from the small lamp on his desk. There was a yellow legal pad in front of him with a list of things that needed to be done—orders that needed to be issued, troop movements that needed to be coordinated.

He had arranged for the movement of a Mike Force company from Moc Hoa north to Duc Bang. Helicopters from the Crusaders would make the transfer about noon. That would give Gerber and his people time to get to the hamlet and prepare.

He had also arranged for several Special Forces men to be transferred from their current assignments to MACV-SOG for a period not to exceed one month. The names on the list provided by Fetterman had given him guidance: Sully Smith, Justin Tyme, T. J. Washington and Galvin Bocker would all be at Tan Son Nhut in the morning. Derek Kepler couldn't make it to Tan Son Nhut, so he was to report to MACV. And finally, there was Andy Santini. He'd deploy from Nha Trang. He'd either have to get himself out to the hamlet, or he'd have to come to Saigon first. Padgett had given him the option on that.

With those items checked off, he'd already made a big dent. Now it was a question of lining up the construction equipment and supplies. The Navy would be of some help. A call to an admiral had gotten him a Seabee unit. Army aviation was supplying the transport.

Padgett sat back and locked his fingers behind his head. Being a general made it very easy to get things done. The old sergeants who controlled the supply functions, the operations and the asset scheduling activities had been in the service so long that a call from a general officer impressed them. They leaped to comply with his instructions. The draftees couldn't have cared less.

Padgett rocked forward and picked up his pipe. He pulled a small knife from his pocket and cleaned the bowl, scraping the burnt tobacco into the overflowing ashtray. He filled his pipe and lit it. There really wasn't anything else to do except smoke.

There was a knock at the door and Padgett looked up. "Come," he called.

"General," said Collins, "I've taken care of the artillery, advising the closest of the fire support bases that they might be required to support our elements at Duc Bang."

"Good," said Padgett. "Why don't you come on in and have a seat. I think that about takes care of it for the evening. The rest can wait until morning."

Collins entered and sat down. He pulled a pack of cigarettes from his pocket and shook one out, then held it up so Padgett could see it.

"Go ahead and smoke," said the general.

"Thank you, sir." Collins used a worn Zippo lighter and snapped it shut. Before he dropped it into his pocket, he rubbed the crest on it.

"I've got a question," said Collins. "Or rather a problem. I don't understand the significance of Duc Bang. The concept makes sense, but the drive for this specific hamlet doesn't make sense. There are others just like it, but no one seems to care about them."

Padgett puffed on his pipe for a moment. "That's how it is in the world of war. A town, a bridge, an open field takes on significance because it seems that the enemy is interested in it. It might not have any strategic significance, other than the enemy's interest." He took his pipe from between his lips and pointed the stem at Collins.

"Look at the Battle of Gettysburg. You had two armies maneuvering in the eastern United States, but neither knew where the other was. They were out there like a couple of blind men, staggering around, waving their hands in the air, searching. Then a rebel regiment entered Gettysburg searching for shoes and stumbled across a federal unit in the area. Within hours a major battle took place, not because Gettysburg was strategically significant, but because both armies were close enough to it to fight and had found each other. When it was over, both sides withdrew from Gettysburg.''

"Which means that Duc Bang, by itself, has no significance, but since the VC seem interested, we're interested."

"That's about the size of it. Throughout history, you'll find examples of that—places that gained importance because the two armies blundered into each other."

Collins leaned forward and flicked his ashes into the tray on the general's desk. "But the enemy already came out to fight during Tet. This seems redundant. Unnecessary."

"That's where policy gets in the way," said Padgett. "If it was up to me, I'd abandon the place, destroy everything that we can't take so that the enemy can't use it, and let Charlie have the empty ground."

"I can't believe you want to avoid a fight, General," said Collins.

"I'm trying to avoid wasting men's lives. There's nothing there that we have to fight to hold. It's not a strategic hilltop, it's not a supply route or a port. The village isn't even worth it."

"The proximity to the Ho Chi Minh Trail and the Cambodian border," said Collins, remembering the briefing he had given that afternoon.

"Yes, that's the little chestnut we pull out when we need a convenient answer. If we're that interested in the Ho Chi Minh Trail, then we should make the effort to stop the supplies farther to the north, and not let anything filter down to this region."

"Then what's it all for?" Collins had forgotten about his cigarette.

"Damned if I know, son. I've been through three of these things now. The Nazis and the Japanese had to be stopped. They presented a clear and present danger. Hitler had announced that he was going to dominate the world and was trying to do it through force of arms. Japan was doing everything it could to conquer Asia. Might have been interesting to see what would have happened when the two sides met, but that wasn't to be. Hitler had to be stopped."

"The Communists say the same thing."

"Right, but they also say that the West will collapse from internal decay. They do not present the clear and present danger that Hitler did. They are dangerous, no question, but not in the same way that Hitler was."

"And Korea?" Collins prompted.

Padgett rocked back in his chair and looked at the ceiling. "Our first war under the Department of Defense, and the first we didn't win. That was a clear aggression against an ally. Oh, the lines might have been a little smudged, North Korea against South Korea, but one army did invade another country. Our goal was to stop the invasion. Not to defeat the North Koreans, but to stop their invasion."

"So in Vietnam we have..."

"A civil war?" asked Padgett, shrugging. "Hell, I don't know. We have Vietcong who are South Vietnamese fighting the government of other South Vietnamese. We have the North Vietnamese helping the Vietcong, with more than just supplies, with soldiers. A civil war that has expanded, but not with the full-scale invasion that happened in Korea."

Collins put out his cigarette and didn't speak. He didn't know what to say.

"You're stunned, right?" said Padgett.

"Well, General, you are talking heresy here. Not the official line at all."

"That's right, and if you carry any of this outside this room, you'll find yourself in the field as a sergeant." Padgett grinned.

Collins reached into his pocket again and worked a cigarette out. He didn't light it, just hung on to it so that he'd have something to do with his hands. "How much support are we going to give to the people at Duc Bang?"

Padgett stared at the younger man. "Don't let my lecture fool you. Policy is that we do everything to defend that hamlet and deny it to the Communists, so that's exactly what we do. We don't buck policy unless we determine that those making the policy have overlooked a vital piece of information. We then inform them of their error and step back to see if the information makes any difference to them."

"But you said that the hamlet has no significance."

"In and of itself," Padgett corrected him. "The enemy has given it some and our policy makers have given it more. Besides, it's as good a place to fight as any."

"Is that what it comes down to?"

Padgett shook his head, a half grin on his face. "All too often, that's exactly what it comes down to. Unfortunately, we don't get to pick the place for the fight."

GERBER, FETTERMAN AND KIT sat at a small table against one wall of the restaurant on the third floor of the Carasel Hotel. It was a dinner restaurant, with white cloths on the tables, red linen napkins, silverware and crystal. The chairs were big and padded and there was a thick carpet on the floor. There were lamps on the walls that looked as if they had been gaslights once and then converted to electricity. A massive chandelier hung from the middle of the ceiling. French doors lined one wall and gave a view of the night lights of Saigon below. The noise of the street, the sounds of rock music and the horns from traffic filtered in.

Gerber sat with his back to the wall, watching the people around him. For some reason he no longer felt like a participant in the activities. He thought of himself as an observer, almost as if he was a journalist recording all that he saw for history. The feeling made no sense to him, and yet he found himself studying the people.

Kit sat to his left, her elbows on the table. She had shifted her chair so that she was closer to Gerber, but was talking to Fetterman. As she spoke, she rubbed the back of Gerber's calf with her foot.

Fetterman sat opposite Gerber, his back to the French doors. Gerber had once asked Fetterman if it bothered him to sit with his back to the door and the master sergeant had said, "Not with you covering me."

"What's on tap for you now, Kit?" Fetterman asked.

"I don't know. Sergeant Santini at Nha Trang has asked that I go there to help with the interrogation of prisoners. They have more than a hundred North Vietnamese and even more Vietcong. He thinks I might be able to do something to help out."

Gerber had no doubt that she would be able to do something. Being in the same room with her would do something to them. There was something electrical about her. Some aura, some texture that made her a noticeable woman. And she was clever. She picked up on the undercurrents in a relationship or a conversation quickly.

"When would you be going?" asked Gerber.

She turned toward him and smiled. "Not for a week or more. Sergeant Santini talked to me today but said that something was brewing so he wasn't sure when he might be free. He might be called out."

Gerber looked at Fetterman and raised an eyebrow. Santini seemed to be talking out of school. He shouldn't have mentioned that there was something else brewing. But then, he had no reason to suspect that Kit wasn't everything she claimed to be. He'd had to tell her something. It just seemed that everything being done in Vietnam hit against the security for the upcoming mission. He wondered if there wasn't a leak that he should try to plug.

"Then there are no real plans," said Gerber.

"No, Mack, I'm going to be here for a few more days." She smiled at him and rocked back in her chair. She drew her arms to the rear so that the fabric of her blouse stretched across her chest. Her top button was undone now, revealing the soft, smooth skin of her throat.

The waitress arrived before any of them had studied the menu. Gerber fell back on his favorite meal of a steak, rare, baked potato and peas. Fetterman ordered the same and Kit opted for seafood.

When the waitress was gone, Fetterman asked, "After we eat, what would you like to do?"

Kit closed her eyes as she thought about it. She grinned at Fetterman. "What I'd *like* to do is probably somewhat different than what I'll *get* to do, so I'll leave everything up to you."

"I think," Gerber said, "that after dinner, I'll head back to the hotel. There's a little paperwork that needs to be finished."

"Oh, no, Mack, that just won't do." She reached up and nervously fingered another button on her blouse until it came undone. She pretended that she didn't notice it. When she turned slightly to speak to Fetterman, Gerber caught a glimpse of the swell of her breast and the white, lacy bra she wore. She had to be aware of that, too.

Fetterman came to Gerber's rescue then. "Maybe we should all just go back to the hotel. I'm tired and could use a good night's sleep."

Kit looked from one to the other. "If I didn't know better, I'd think that the two of you had something to do in the morning."

"We do," said Gerber. "We've a meeting with some brass hats at USARV about the conduct of the war. I know I'm looking forward to it."

He felt her foot on his leg again but she had slipped off her shoe so that she could massage his calf with her toes. He wondered how she could sit there so calmly, look so innocent, and be working so hard to seduce him.

Loyalty, he told himself, was the name of the game. Robin might not be at the table, but she was in Vietnam. He owed her something. The philosophy of loving the one you were with was not one that he subscribed to. Except that neither he nor Robin had made any long-range commitments. They had talked of their feelings and their plans, but had made no mutual plans. It might have been the war, or the situation, or a hundred other things.

He reached under the table and seized Kit's foot, trying to push it away. Instead she leaned back and sighed as if his touch was the most pleasant experience in the world.

Across the table, Fetterman was grinning like the biggest Buddha in the world. He seemed to know everything that was going on.

"You plan all this, Tony?" Gerber asked.

Fetterman touched his chest and looked innocent. "I'm afraid I don't know what you mean."

"Maybe I should try to call Robin again," he said, but made no move to get up. He still held Kit's foot and she was wiggling her toes so that they massaged his wrist.

Gerber let go of her foot. He raised both his hands and rubbed his face, noticing that he was sweating heavily. He didn't think the air temperature had anything to do with it. By shifting slightly in his chair, he could see Kit's thigh. She was sitting so that he had a full view of her leg if he wanted it. He told himself that he didn't, but he looked at her every chance he got.

"Robin's been working very hard," he said.

"Maybe too hard," Kit suggested.

And then the food arrived, saving Gerber for a moment. The waitress put a plate in front of each person, smiled at the three and asked, "You want more?"

"Everything's fine," said Gerber.

They ate in silence for a few moments. Gerber thought about Kit. She would take any relationship with him that she could get. She was aware of Robin, but didn't care. It might be that Kit believed their backgrounds were so different that she could not have a long-lasting relationship with Gerber. The thing was, given the war, there was a real atmosphere of taking what you could while you could because there might not be a tomorrow. Many people that Gerber knew, men and women both, subscribed to it.

But Gerber felt a loyalty to Morrow. She had been with him through some of the roughest times. Gerber stopped eating and set down his fork, realizing suddenly what he was doing. He was giving himself all the reasons that he should ignore Kit. What he should really be doing was relaxing and enjoying himself because he'd be in the field the next day.

"Something wrong?" asked Fetterman.

"No, not at all."

Kit smiled at him and he felt her foot on his leg again. This time he didn't try to remove it. He would enjoy the situation, but find a way to keep Kit from following him to his room.

"No," he repeated. "Nothing at all." He picked up his fork to eat his dinner.

7

HOTEL THREE, TAN SON NHUT, SAIGON

The jeep dropped them off close to the gate for Hotel Three. As soon as they were out, with their gear and weapons, the driver slammed the jeep into first and roared off, as if afraid of the coming dawn. The air policeman standing at the gate, looking as if he'd been asleep a moment before, waved them through.

Gerber shouldered his gear, his ruck and pistol belt with the three canteens on it and his weapon, an M-16. He had several bandoliers of ammo for it. Fetterman had done the same and carried an M-16, having left his M-3A1 grease gun behind. Carrying it sometimes created a logistical problem that he didn't want to face. Besides, a well-maintained M-16 wouldn't jam. The press had done a number on it, too.

They walked past the World's Largest PX and the movie theater that was showing the latest in film from the World, and around the corner of the chain link fence that protected Hotel Three. The gate there was open and light was bleeding out from the terminal building tucked under the control tower.

Gerber moved toward it and dropped his gear just inside the door, keeping his hand on his weapon. After Tet, with the Communists in the wire and overrunning part of the airfield, everyone hung on to his weapon.

Inside was a plywood counter painted green and behind that was a scheduling board painted white. A bored Spec 5 sat behind the counter sleeping. The floor was dirty plywood, and to the right were several chairs and tables, some of them holding magazines.

"Morning, Captain," said a voice.

Gerber turned. "Damn! Justin. Didn't see you there? How in the hell are you?"

And then he looked at the others—Sully Smith who'd been in the World longer than any of them, along with Galvin Bocker and Thomas Jefferson Washington.

Gerber moved forward, shaking hands with the men he hadn't seen in over a year and then with those he hadn't seen for a couple of weeks. "Damn," he repeated, "it's good to see you all again. Just like old times. Sully, you finally dragged your ass out of the World."

Smith grinned broadly. Smith was a short, stocky man with a dusky complexion. He was half Italian and half American and was originally from Ohio, where he had spent his Saturdays rooting on Ohio State.

"This is my third tour, Captain," he reminded Gerber. "They let me stay home a little longer than the rest of you neophytes."

"Good to have you back," said Gerber.

Smith's grin seemed to broaden as he said, "I suppose you know that Ohio State smashed Iowa the last time they met. Wasn't a fair fight at all."

"I won't hold that against you," said Gerber.

Smith turned toward Fetterman and shook the master sergeant's hand. "Nice to see you again, Master Sergeant."

"Glad to see you," said Fetterman.

Gerber moved to Washington. He was a large black man who towered over many of the Americans and dwarfed the Vietnamese. He had been the junior medical specialist on Gerber's old team, taking the top spot when Ian McMillan was killed.

"Welcome aboard, T.J.," said Gerber.

"Glad to be back here," said Washington. "Spent my time getting some additional training."

"Great," said Gerber. "We'll probably need it." He then nodded to Bocker. "Galvin."

"Sir."

Gerber moved to one of the chairs and sat down. The men crowded around him, Fetterman dropping into one of the other chairs with Tyme kneeling on the floor in front of him.

"Can't tell you much about this, here," he said, gesturing at the open nature of the terminal building. "Chopper should be in here to deploy us in about fifteen minutes. Sorry to get you all up so early in the morning."

"Where are we going, exactly?" asked Tyme.

"Small village north of Tay Ninh." He looked at the Spec 5 behind the counter who seemed to be even more bored than before. Gerber pulled a map from his pocket, opened it and then refolded it so that Duc Bang was in the center. He pointed at it. "There."

"Shit," Bocker said.

"That about sums it up," said Gerber.

"Anyone have a good reason for sticking us way out in the boonies like that?" asked Smith.

"Not one that I've heard. Everyone seems to think it's a good idea, though."

"Yeah," said Washington. "I remember some of those other good ideas that people've had."

Gerber glanced at Fetterman. "Anything you want to say before we blast out of here, Tony?"

Fetterman rubbed his face, as if to chase the last of the sleep from his body. "Think of this as putting in a camp, just like when we built the old Triple Nickel. Same breakdown of areas of responsibility and coordination."

"We start patrolling as soon as we get there?" asked Tyme.

"Gentlemen," said Gerber, holding up a hand, "this is not the place to get into this. My understanding is that the LZ will be cold. There are troops on the ground."

"American or Vietnamese?" asked Smith.

"American. Last radio contact was just after midnight. Some light contact. Harassing fire, actually. We land just after dawn so we shouldn't have a problem there."

"Sir," began Washington.

"I don't want to cut you off, T.J., but the less said here, the better we're going to be in the field. We should be able to have a detailed briefing when we hit the ground. I know you don't like this, but it's the way the situation broke. If there was something I thought you should know, I'd tell you. Not here, but once we were airborne—but there just isn't anything."

Fetterman took over then. "Once we're on the ground, everyone will have a better feel for what's happening. Supplies have been arranged and will be arriving for us. It's all coordinated through another office. Not ours."

Each of the men understood exactly what that meant. MACV-SOG understood how the Special Forces worked and would supply everything they needed. Conventional army units tended to send things the brass hats thought the men would need, not necessarily what they actually needed. Each of them had heard helicopter pilots complaining about the standard load for their .38-caliber revolvers. Twenty-one rounds, a carryover from the three magazines issued with the

.45 auto. It meant they could reload two and one-half times. Conventional Army thinking applied to an unconventional circumstance.

"Which means we should remain flexible," said Washington.

"Extremely flexible," Fetterman said.

There was a pop of rotor blades in the distance. The clerk sat upright suddenly, as if shot, and glanced at the men in the terminal, seeing them for the first time.

"Go back to sleep," said Gerber. "That'll be for us."

"Yes, sir," said the clerk. "No problem."

Without a word, the men moved toward the door. Gerber shouldered his equipment again. He glanced over his shoulder and saw the team spread out, each with his own gear, specialized for his function—Bocker with the radio, Washington with his first-aid kit that contained more than the standard bag and Sully Smith with his demolitions gear. They stood there silently, watching as the helicopter approached from the north, the nav lights winking dully in the increasing brightness of the rising sun. At first it was nothing more than a speck, but that changed until it took on the unmistakable shape of a UH-1.

The aircraft crossed over the World's Largest PX and landed on the grass of Hotel Three, flattening it under the rotor wash. As it settled to the ground, bouncing once or twice, Gerber, holding his beret on his head, ran out to it. The crew chief jumped from behind his M-60 machine gun, taking the rucksack from Gerber's hand. He tossed it into the cargo compartment, jamming it up next to the seat of the AC.

Gerber climbed into the back and sat down on the red canvas troop seat. He slid to the far side, just in front of the door gunner. Fetterman was next, followed by the rest of the men. The crew chief made sure that the men were sitting on the troop seat or on the floor, and that the equipment was up toward the front to balance the load. When he had everyone inside the aircraft and the load distributed to his satisfaction, he climbed into his well, holding a thumb up.

They came to a hover and lifted off, heading to the south. They turned to the west and lost altitude until they were only a few feet off the ground. The sun was behind them now, rising faster. The ground was bathed in shadows and bright spots, the features changing from a charcoal to light gray and finally filling with bright, vivid colors.

Once they were beyond the approach paths to Tan Son Nhut, they popped up to altitude and Gerber leaned to the right, looking down at Vietnam. The pilot's axiom, never walk when you can ride and never ride when you can fly, seemed to be more true now. A convoy was stopped on Highway One, the lead truck burning brightly, the thick black smoke curling into the morning air. They had hit a mine, Gerber was sure. Too many of the GIs were standing around watching the truck burn. If it had been an ambush, there would have been shooting and no one standing around.

The chopper broke away from the highway, turning toward the northwest, crossing above the Hobo Woods and then west of Dau Tieng where the Michelin Rubber Plantation provided cover for the VC and the NVA. The plantation buildings, constructed by the French, were now part of an American complex. Gerber had been there once, surprised by the huge aboveground swimming pool and the little hootch where he bought soft-serve ice cream.

With that, Gerber's mind slipped back to the previous evening. Fetterman had enjoyed himself as Gerber tried to avoid Kit's attempts to seduce him. Fetterman had kept making suggestions so that he could leave the two of them alone, but Gerber hadn't allowed it.

Finally they had gone back to the hotel and Fetterman had said he was going to his room for a few minutes. That left

Gerber with Kit in the hotel lobby. Every few moments, she suggested they go to his room, but Gerber refused. She finally persuaded him to go upstairs, telling him they could call Fetterman from his room.

Once they were inside the door, Kit threw herself at Gerber, her arms around his neck as she kissed him. Gerber responded automatically, his back against the door. He broke the kiss and looked over her shoulder, sure that Robin would be inside somewhere, but she wasn't. Some of her things were still there, but Robin was missing.

Kit danced away from him then, smiling broadly. She sat on the bed and patted it, trying to get him to sit beside her. She had crossed her legs, letting her skirt ride high. She leaned back on her hands, throwing out her chest.

Gerber stood across the room, at first watching her, and then looking at the things left behind by Robin. The room was suddenly filled by Robin.

Kit fingered her blouse, slowly unbuttoning it. Gerber watched as she finished and slipped it from her shoulders. With it gone, she pulled up her skirt so that her black, lace panties were visible.

For a moment, Gerber had been tempted. Sorely tempted, but it wouldn't be fair to Robin. She'd never know. And then he'd shaken his head.

Kit had understood immediately and put her blouse back on. She got off the bed and moved to Gerber, kissing him again. She rubbed herself against him, slowly, and then stepped away.

"Maybe later," was all she said.

She left then, still smiling, and Gerber almost called her back. He even reached for the doorknob, but then locked it instead of opening the door, taking pride in his willpower. As he reached the bed, he decided that willpower wasn't all it was cracked up to be.

Now, as they passed east of Tay Ninh West, a small Special Forces camp with a single short runway inside the wire, Gerber wiped the thoughts of Kit from his mind. Close didn't count, except with hand grenades. He figured that someone was putting him in for the Good Conduct Medal. The sun was now rising higher until all of the ground was bright and the last bit of night had been chased away. Through the cockpit windshield was an almost unbroken sea of green that marked the beginning of the triple canopy jungle that extended north to the Central Highlands, where it became so thick that progress through it was marked in yards per day rather than miles an hour.

In the distance was the huge clearing where Duc Bang was slowly emerging from an early morning ground mist. Gerber saw the settlement and turned, touching the door gunner on the arm. He motioned the man close and then shouted over the sound of the engine, "See if the pilot can talk to anyone on the ground there. Make sure the LZ is cold."

The man held up a thumb and nodded. He rocked back, forcing himself into the corner of his well and squeezed the little black box for the intercom. A moment later, he pushed his face close to Gerber and yelled, "No problem on the ground. Some sniper fire during the night, but nothing for the past three hours."

Gerber nodded and turned to Fetterman, passing the word. "Sniper fire last night. Let's not give Charlie an easy target."

Fetterman nodded and passed the word.

Gerber continued to watch the clearing. As they neared it, a plume of yellow smoke began to grow and by sighting on it, Gerber spotted the hamlet. Just a smudge behind the smoke. They began a long, slow letdown to the edge of the village.

Over the roar of the rotors, the engine and the wind, Gerber shouted, "Everyone out as quickly as possible and hit the deck. We'll take stock and then move toward the ville. Questions?"

When no one spoke, Gerber nodded. He chambered a round and made sure that the safety was on. He wanted to reach for his rucksack and put it on, but it was buried under the other equipment. They would toss it all out the door when they were on the ground. If the LZ was cold, they could collect it and then climb the berm. If it was hot, the equipment could wait.

But all that became academic. As they neared, Gerber saw that the smoke was coming from inside the hamlet, marking the helipad just inside the berm, on the side of the village away from the tree lines. It was more than two hundred yards to the nearest place the VC could hide, and it was protected by the berm and the village.

"Looks good," shouted Fetterman.

They flared then and settled to the ground. As the skids touched the pad, Gerber was out the door. He spun to get the equipment, but that was being shoved out the other side by Sully Smith and Galvin Bocker. A dozen grunts were on the berm, watching the show, but their weapons were pointed toward the empty fields.

In seconds there was a blast of wind as the rotors took a deeper bite of the air. The chopper rose, hesitated and then shot off, only a couple of feet above the ground. The rotor wash trailed it, flattening the elephant grass and the rice plants in its wake. The noise faded slowly until it was quiet.

One of the grunts appeared, standing beside Gerber, looking down at him. "I'm Helmsman," he said.

Gerber got to his feet but didn't shake hands. The VC looked for things like that, and although they were six or seven hundred yards from the jungle on that side of the hamlet, a sniper with a good rifle could hit them.

"Gerber. What's the situation?" He glanced at Fetterman, who was already getting the equipment picked up. A couple of the grunts appeared to help.

"Harassment fire all night. Mortars early and then snipers. Pump a few rounds into the hamlet and then vanish quickly."

"You send out patrols?"

Helmsman glanced at the black captain bars sewn to the collar of Gerber's jungle jacket. "No, sir. I've only a platoon and thought it better that I stay here. I didn't want to divide my force so that we could be chopped up piecemeal."

Fetterman was beginning to move off the pad and into the hamlet. Gerber nodded and said, "Let's follow them."

"Yes, sir." Helmsman waited for Gerber to move and then dropped in behind him. "I know we should have gone out after the VC, but I didn't have the manpower to do it."

"You call in artillery?"

"Not during the night. Stragglers began to filter in, villagers returning home, and I didn't know where they were. The snipers weren't doing any harm, so I didn't call for the arty. If things had gotten worse, then, maybe."

They passed between two hootches and entered the main part of the hamlet. The interior seemed to be slightly depressed, as if to protect it from an enemy on the ground outside it. With the buildings between him and the trees, Gerber felt more comfortable. He looked at the young officer. "I'm not criticizing your decisions, just getting all the information. You might have been right. Now, any way to get some hot coffee?"

"We didn't want to start any fires until it was daylight and we were waiting for the Vietnamese to light the first ones."

"Trying not to draw attention to yourself?"

"Yes, sir."

Fetterman appeared at their sides and said, "Got everything off the pad. Thought we'd store most of it in the arms locker."

"Arms locker lost its roof and one side is down. The villagers have been using it and we have a reporter in there for the protection it would offer."

"Christ!" Gerber snapped. "That's all we need is a fucking reporter out here."

"She seems to be a good sort," said Helmsman.

"She?" Gerber echoed. "What's her name?"

"Robin Morrow."

Gerber didn't know if he should laugh or shout. The last thing he wanted was to find a reporter on the scene of what was supposed to be a semisecret mission. No one had told him that he shouldn't mention it to reporters, but then, no one had told him that he should. Now, his appearance with a team of several Special Forces soldiers, about to be reinforced with a strike company from the Mike Force at Moc Hoa, was going to cause questions.

"Where is she now?"

"I suspect she's sleeping in the arms locker. She wasn't supposed to be here last night, but she came on the last chopper."

"You could have sent her out this morning."

"Yes, sir," said Helmsman, "but I figured she could go out with us when we left later."

There was a double pop in the field and Gerber dropped to one knee. Helmsman dived to the ground, holding his steel pot in place with both hands.

"Incoming!"

Gerber saw Fetterman running across the hamlet, Tyme right behind him. They leaped an overturned fifty-five-gallon drum and dropped to the berm. Fetterman was scanning the tree line with binoculars.

The first round hit, far short of the perimeter. It exploded harmlessly in a rice paddy, throwing up a fountain of brown water and sewage-soaked mud. The second round fell closer, but did no damage other than taking out a small section of one dike.

"Harassment fire," said Gerber. He stood up and stared into the trees. Mortars were such lousy weapons that he figured one day they'd kill him. He had no respect for them. The VC's 60 mm mortar was too small for anything but harassment. It could destroy a truck if the round hit it in the engine, and the shrapnel would kill a dozen men if they were close enough, but they rarely were. The enemy was lucky to be able to hit a village, and mud would eliminate any killing effect. Gerber knew men who had been next to mortar rounds that had detonated, and their only complaint was a ringing in the ears from the noise of the explosion.

There were three more pops, but Gerber didn't see the tube. Again he dropped to one knee, staying close to the mud wall of the hootch for a little added protection.

Again the rounds exploded outside the perimeter. Fetterman pointed and Tyme nodded. As the last of the mortars detonated, Fetterman was on his feet.

"Sir, we've got the tube spotted. Justin and I would like to go after it."

"Won't be there when you get out there, Tony."

"We can find the trail."

Gerber turned to Helmsman. "You want a couple of your people to go along?"

Helmsman hesitated before speaking. "Sure. I'll get together with Sergeant Warren and form a squad."

"Let's move it, sir," said Fetterman. "The VC are probably breaking down the tube now to move it. We'll need to hurry."

As the lieutenant spun to find his men, Gerber asked, "You sure this is a good idea?"

"Why not?" Fetterman asked. "At the very least, we'll show the Vietcong that we're coming out to engage them. It'll make them think twice about dropping mortars in here."

"Don't get too far afield because we won't be able to offer support, and you'll be going out with men we don't know."

"They're American soldiers, sir. They'll be just fine."

"Check with Galvin for a radio and keep in touch."

"Yes, sir."

Helmsman returned and said, "Third squad will go out with you."

Fetterman nodded. "We'll need to coordinate the radio procedures and frequencies."

"No problem."

The men came straggling from the center of the hamlet. They were a dirty, tired-looking bunch. They carried their weapons as if they had no respect for them. One man held his by the barrel, dragging the butt in the dirt. Two others had their weapons draped over their shoulders. Only about half the men had bothered to lock and load.

Gerber watched the men assemble and then stepped close to Fetterman. "I've seen Yards and strikers looking sharper."

"Matter of training, Captain. We'll be able to teach them something."

"Then go," said Gerber.

Fetterman turned and walked over to the men. He didn't want to line them up for inspection, because that would make everyone a target. He crouched in front of them and spoke quietly.

"We're going to assault the tree line and we're going to do it by the book. Once inside the trees, we'll sweep through, looking for signs that the VC are around. If we find any, we'll give chase until they either leave the AO or we find and engage them."

They were all quiet, and Fetterman continued. "Take only spare ammo, grenades, water and a first-aid kit. I want the weapons loaded and on safe. We move out in three minutes."

Tyme joined them and moved among the men, checking weapons and packs and telling them what to leave behind. Bocker stood at the rear, a PRC-25 at his feet.

"Tony, this might not be the best idea in the world. We could call for helicopters and keep them on station for a while. Might be a better way of operating."

"Hell, Captain, Charlie's already seen us getting ready to move out. He'll either have taken off and we won't find him, or he'll fire on us and we'll have a chance to take him out."

"Let's not get ambushed by stupidity," said Gerber.

"No problem, sir. I know what I'm doing."

"Then get going."

"Yes, sir." He turned. "Sergeant Tyme, take the point and head for the trees. When you're halfway there, let us catch up and we'll move forward on line."

Tyme headed out, crossing the berm and then a rice paddy dike. The men spread out behind him, following in his footsteps.

"Good luck, Tony, and don't take any chances."

"No, sir. See you in a couple of hours."

"Right."

Fetterman joined the rear of the formation, watching the grunts as they crossed into the open. As they began the patrol, he noticed a sudden change in them. They realized that their lives now depended on being good soldiers.

Maybe it won't be so bad after all, thought Fetterman.

8

THE HAMLET OF DUC BANG, REPUBLIC OF VIETNAM

The sound of the incoming chopper woke Morrow. Corporal Russell had loaned her a poncho liner to use as a blanket. The concrete floor of the arms locker was uncomfortable, and she had been sure she heard rats scrambling over the rubble, but hadn't had the courage to look. She'd pretended she couldn't hear it, squeezing her eyes shut, sure that she wouldn't be able to sleep. The next thing she knew, a helicopter was coming closer, waking her.

She threw off the poncho liner and stood up, stretching. Her mouth tasted like the rats had nested there while she was asleep. She stooped, picked up her camera bag and wished she could find five minutes of privacy. She wished she could brush her teeth with cold water and take a bath in hot. There were times when she wished she had decided on a career that demanded a little less personal sacrifice.

She stumbled from the arms locker into a dull gray morning with a mist hanging in the air, making everything sticky and hard to see. For the first time she was cold, surprised that the tropical air could hold a chill. In the distance, she saw the chopper, first sitting on the ground, a vague shape with flashing lights, and then lifting into the air. As it disappeared, she noticed that a half dozen Vietnamese women had gathered around a cooking fire. She walked over and crouched near them.

There had been a quiet babble of voices as she approached, but they fell silent, looking at her with hooded eyes. The oldest of the women was stirring the bubbling water in a black pot with a big stick.

"English?" asked Morrow. "Any of you speak English?"

They all looked at her but none of them spoke. It didn't mean that they couldn't speak English, just that they wouldn't. At least to her.

For a few minutes, she sat, watching them prepare the breakfast of rice and fish. The women remained silent, saying only those things necessary to finish the preparations for the meal. Morrow wondered if they were afraid of her or if they hated her. There was a hostility in the air that she couldn't quite place. When it was evident that the women weren't going to talk, Morrow stood and left.

As she moved through the hamlet, there was a quiet double pop and someone shouting, "Incoming!" Morrow glanced around, found she was too far from the arms locker to return there and dived for cover near the mud wall of a partially destroyed hootch.

The two explosions in the field outside the hamlet were far from frightening. Morrow sat up and saw that the women were still sitting around their fire as if nothing had happened. She shouted at them and they looked back at her, but the warning was not understood.

There were three more pops. Morrow rolled against the side of the hootch and listened for the explosions. She worried that the women behind her would be killed, but didn't know what to do for them.

The detonations came from outside the hamlet. As soon as the mortars had exploded, men ran through the area. A squad of them formed and moved toward the perimeter. Morrow saw them, ghostly shapes in the morning mist. She thought about joining them and then decided she'd rather study the reactions of the Vietnamese. They seemed curiously unafraid of the incoming fire.

Morrow stood there quietly, watching the squad form and move out, first a single man on the point followed by the rest of the patrol. The mist was thinning. They hurried across the open rice paddies.

She saw the two officers watching the men and then recognized them. She stood there for a moment, surprised, and then rushed forward, forgetting her camera bag.

"Mack," she shouted as she approached.

Gerber spun and looked at her. "Robin. So this is where you got to."

Helmsman watched them and asked, "You two know each other?"

"We've seen each other once or twice here and there," said Gerber. He stared at her for a moment and added, "She's got more time in-country than about any four GIs you'd care to name. More combat time than most of them, too. And to make it worse, she's a volunteer."

Helmsman studied her with new eyes. "Really?"

"Not really," she said, but she was grinning broadly.

"Let's get out of the open," said Gerber. He saw Bocker hanging around the rear of the group and ordered, "Galvin, I want you to raise Santini as he's coming in, and divert him to Moc Hoa. He can coordinate the strike company. And keep in touch with Fetterman."

Bocker nodded. "Yes, sir. Morning, Miss Morrow."

"Sergeant Bocker. How are you?"

"Fine, ma'am. You're looking particularly good today."

"Well, thank you, but I don't believe you."

Sully Smith appeared then and reported, "No damage in the hamlet. Or rather no fresh damage. Everything landed in the fields on the outside." He stopped talking and stared at Morrow.

"Sully Smith, isn't it?" she said. "Haven't seen you in a long time."

Smith looked at Gerber and then at Morrow, confused. He remembered Karen Morrow, the flight nurse that Gerber had been friendly with, but this woman didn't look quite right. He'd seen Robin a couple of times, but was confused since it had all been over a year earlier.

Gerber rescued him. "Sully, you must remember Robin."

"Of course, I do." He held out a hand. "Miss Morrow? What are you doing here?"

Gerber interrupted before she could reply. "That's a good question. What *are* you doing here?"

"Right now, I'm being overwhelmed. They give you your old team back sometime in the past two days?"

"No," said Gerber. "It's a little more complicated than that. Lieutenant, if anyone around here has some coffee, I think we'd all like a cup, especially if we don't have to stand out here where we're good targets."

"Yes, sir," said Helmsman. "I would imagine that one of the squads will have something cooking."

Letting Helmsman lead them, they left the open area at the edge of the hamlet, heading toward the center. They passed the group of women who still sat at their pot, still stirring the contents and still ignoring everything else.

They found a squad sitting around a fire of their own, a steel pot being used to boil water. As the men started to get to their feet at the appearance of the officer, Gerber waved at them, motioning them down.

"Coffee, sir?" one of them asked.

Gerber produced his canteen cup. "If there's enough for everyone else." When he'd been given some, he looked up at Morrow. "You didn't tell me what you're doing here."

She grinned broadly. "Neither did you."

THE PATROL DIDN'T USE the rice paddy dikes, though that would have been the quickest way to the tree line. Instead, they walked through the center of the paddies, stepping on the plants to keep their feet from sinking deeply into the muck. As they neared the tree line, they fanned out in a row, then swept forward rapidly, not giving the enemy a chance to set up an ambush.

At the edge of the trees, Tyme halted, as did the others. He crouched there, searching the light brush for signs of the enemy, searching for signs of the mortar tube. It was quiet in the trees. There were no birds squawking and no monkeys chattering. Both were bad omens, suggesting the enemy was near.

Tyme stood, then moved forward, avoiding a small fern and a larger bush with thick, green leaves. He stopped next to a coconut tree, his rifle at the ready. Around him the line began to collapse inward as the men pulled together to support one another in the jungle.

Tyme glanced to his right. Fetterman was anchoring the line there, but Tyme couldn't see him. Two soldiers were visible, but now they were in the field, they seemed to understand what they were doing. Their noise discipline was good, and they held their weapons at the ready as they searched for the enemy.

The left side was doing the same, anchored by the platoon sergeant. The men were all working together in a coordinated fashion. If someone took the time to teach them a little military discipline at the camps, they would turn into a crack unit. Then Tyme drove those thoughts from his mind, and began the search for the enemy tube.

In three minutes, he found the firing site. The enemy appeared to have been there for most of the night; the grass was flattened, suggesting they had slept there. They found a single AK round and nothing else.

As he entered the zone, Tyme touched the shoulders of the men closest to him, establishing the security. When Fetterman appeared a moment later, there was nothing for him to do but examine the ground where the mortar tube had been positioned.

"I make it no more than five minutes," he said.

Tyme nodded his agreement and pointed to the west. "Went that way."

"Down the long axis of the tree line, of course," said Fetterman. The foliage wasn't thick, not as it could be elsewhere in Vietnam, but it provided cover for the enemy. He could see no signs of them moving, but that only meant they were at least a hundred yards away. If they hadn't gone more than a klick, Fetterman was sure they could catch them.

"Of course, there's the possibility of ambush," said Fetterman. It wouldn't be the first time the enemy had dropped a few rounds into an area to entice a counter-mortar patrol out to ambush them.

"Want me to take the point?" asked Tyme.

"No," Fetterman said. "I think all we'll do here is search the immediate area and then return to the hamlet."

"They haven't gotten that much of a head start," Tyme said.

"I don't like the feel of this," Fetterman told him. "The smart thing was to set it up so they could take potshots at us as we headed across the paddies, but that would leave them open for artillery and sniping from our end. I think they're trying to draw us farther from our support, out of sight of the hamlet, so they can chop us up."

"My boys are better than they look," said Warren. He hadn't spoken but had listened to the whole conversation.

"I don't mean this to reflect on your boys, Sergeant," said Fetterman. "I just mean that I don't like the feel of it. My philosophy is make the enemy do all the work. We know they've moved the tube and I think that takes care of our mission. We don't have to chase them down."

"Then we head on back?"

"Let's check in and see what they've got for us," said Fetterman.

BOCKER APPEARED at Gerber's elbow and said, "Got a call from a Muleskinner's aircraft. Said he was inbound with a construction team and wanted me to pop smoke."

Gerber looked at Helmsman. "You know anything about that?"

"No, sir."

"What type of aircraft did he have?" Gerber asked.

"Shit hook. He's got a bulldozer slung underneath so he won't be able to use the internal pad."

Gerber took a sip of his coffee, burned his tongue and said, "Shit." He rubbed his chin with his left hand. "Have him land outside the perimeter on the north side. We'll use them to raise the berm slightly and create a shallow moat."

"Yes, sir," said Bocker.

"What's going on?" Robin asked.

"We're in the process of rebuilding this place," said Gerber. "That's one of the reasons I'm here. I've some experience in building a camp in hostile territory. It's part of the strategic hamlet concept."

"That all on the record?"

Gerber felt a knifelike fear knot his stomach. No one had said the mission was a secret one, and once the hamlet was reestablished, it certainly wouldn't be kept under wraps.

"Let's just say it'll be on the record a little later."

"Anyone ask these people what they think about that?"

Now Gerber was puzzled. "You mean ask the Vietnamese?"

"Exactly," said Morrow. "Anyone come out here and ask them if they wanted their village rebuilt as a strategic hamlet."

"Why wouldn't they?" Helmsman asked. "We'll be giving them everything they could possibly want. It'll be better than it was. That's right, isn't it, Captain?"

"We're here to reconstruct the hamlet," said Gerber.

"But the people didn't ask for the help, did they?"

Gerber shrugged. "I guess technically, they didn't. Should that make a difference?"

Morrow glanced at the ground and then turned. The villagers were hovering on the edge, where they could watch the Americans but where they wouldn't be drawn into the conversation.

"Does it look like they want your help?"

"They don't seem to be protesting," Gerber said. "They look frightened, but given the circumstances, that's understandable."

Bocker interrupted them. "Sir, I've got to get out there to throw the smoke for the chopper."

"Then go," said Gerber. He turned to Helmsman. "You might want to get another patrol out in the other section of jungle, until we get the strikers in here. Once the choppers are in, then we can pull in the patrols, at least for today."

"Excuse me, Captain, but I'm supposed to pull out of here today. We didn't plan for an extended stay in the field."

"Let's play this by ear," said Gerber. "I'd like to keep you around, at least until tomorrow. I can coordinate with your headquarters if we need that."

The expression on Helmsman's face changed. He looked angry and then nodded. "Yes, sir."

"I know this is going to be rough on you and your men, but we may need your help to get this thing organized."

"Yes, sir," said Helmsman. He turned and headed toward the rest of his men to organize the patrol.

As he left, Morrow stood up and said, "You didn't answer my question."

Gerber shook his head. "Robin, I have my orders. I can't see where it's going to bother these people. T.J. will look at them and see if they need medical assistance. Food will be brought in. What's the problem?"

"I don't know," she said. "There's something going on here that's not quite right. These people are afraid, as you said, but there's something going on that I don't understand. If Tony's with you, maybe he can help me find out what it is."

"Tony's in the field right now. He'll be back in this morning. Maybe you should take a chopper and get out of here."

"Why?"

Gerber laughed. "Well, I was about to suggest that it's going to be dangerous, but I guess, given everything that's happened in the past, it shouldn't make that much difference."

Smith returned and said, "Captain, I've made a survey of the hamlet."

"Just a second, Sully. Robin, when Tony gets in I'll have him talk to you."

"Okay, Mack." She stood quietly for a moment and then walked off.

Gerber turned to Smith. "What'd you learn on the survey?"

"The damage to the bunker line is fairly superficial. We should be able to make repairs this afternoon and be ready to defend this evening. Once that's accomplished, we can work on repairing the community structures—the school and the dispensary. I made a quick head count. There are about three hundred people here now and, ignoring the women and the old men and children, a labor force of about thirty."

"That's not right," said Gerber. "There should be more young men."

"And women," Smith said. "Everyone of military age is gone. They may be in hiding."

"You sure about the head count?"

"Yes, sir. The people keep moving around, but I've got a fairly accurate one. About three hundred people."

"Seems there are fewer."

"Yes, sir. Seems that way."

Gerber looked at the younger man and then surveyed the hamlet. "You know, Sully, Robin's right. There *is* something going on here."

9

THE HAMLET OF DUC BANG, REPUBLIC OF VIETNAM

The huge Army Chinook had roared out of the sky, a big gray Caterpillar dangling under it. Bocker had walked to the berm and thrown a purple smoke grenade as far into the rice paddies as he could. It landed about twenty-five yards from the perimeter and began to burn, the purple smoke boiling up out of the shallow water.

The helicopter appeared in the east, flying at a thousand feet. It approached slowly, descending toward the smoke until it came to a hover a hundred feet in the air. It settled slowly, while Bocker watched the bulldozer, making sure it wasn't oscillating. Bocker signaled them when the bulldozer was on the ground, and the chopper dropped the sling. It then rose slightly and moved to the right where it landed in another rice paddy. The wash from the twin rotor systems rolled over the paddies like the first breezes of a hurricane, flattening the grass and rice, and forcing the water into the corners of the dikes. Bocker lifted a hand to his helmet, holding it down as he crouched on one knee, his head bowed.

He kept the handset of the radio against his ear, but his eyes were closed against the assault of the rotor-blown debris.

The rear ramp came down and a dozen men ran from the helicopter. They fanned out, away from the chopper as it rose into the sky. It hung there, the roar from the twin turbines drowning out every other sound, the rotors beating the air like the wings of a monstrous bird. Then the aircraft pivoted and the nose dropped slightly as it began to move away from the hamlet. It climbed slowly, as if the effort to gain altitude was beyond its strength.

When the Chinook was gone and the silence had returned, Bocker stood and waved. The men in the field moved toward the bulldozer. They worked to remove the huge straps and net that had been used to support the machine as the chopper carried it from Saigon. As soon as they had it free one man climbed into the seat and started it. There was a deep-throated rumble as black diesel smoke belched from the stack, then silence as the engine stalled with a gasp. The soldier looked off into the distance as he tried to restart it. He got it running again, the engine grunting like some giant animal.

The men swarmed over the beast, and it turned on one tread before beginning its short journey to the camp. It smashed through the flimsy rice paddy dikes, letting all the water mingle. When they were only ten yards from Bocker, at the edge of the berm, the machine stopped and one man hopped down, wading through the water like MacArthur going ashore in the Philippines.

He approached Bocker, glanced at the startled Green Beret and said, "Lieutenant Donald Cramer, United States Navy, reporting as ordered. Is there an officer around here?"

Bocker wasn't sure what to do. The sound of the machinery made communication difficult. He turned and looked for help from the hamlet and saw Gerber heading toward them.

"Over there," said Bocker. "Captain Gerber."

Gerber arrived as the sound of the engine died. "The Sea-bees have arrived," he observed.

"Yes, sir," said Cramer. "What do you want us to do first?"

"That the only equipment you brought?"

Cramer shrugged. "It's the only equipment we have with us now. Building materials are being requisitioned in Saigon and should begin arriving sometime this afternoon."

Gerber studied the Navy officer. He wore neatly tailored, stateside-style fatigues that showed no signs of sweat. He wore a white T-shirt, something a soldier would never do. There was a pistol belt around his waist holding a canteen, a .45 auto and a pouch for his aviator-type sunglasses. A great costume for a Hollywood production, but not for combat.

"Been in Vietnam long?" Gerber asked.

"Six months," said Cramer. "Been working out of Nha Be."

"Okay," said Gerber. "I want the berm around the hamlet about four feet high. Scoop the dirt out of the paddies around it, making a shallow moat. Give us a good field of fire and give Charlie a little hill to climb."

"No problem."

"Maybe you'd like to make a tour with my demolitions man. He's surveyed the hamlet and can give you an idea of what needs to be done."

"Let me brief my chief and I'll be ready."

"One other thing," said Gerber. "We've taken some fire this morning. Harassment mortars. I've one patrol out and we're sending a second. Might want to brief your men that we're not completely secured."

"Aye aye."

As the naval officer ran off to brief his men, Bocker said, "I don't know about him."

"Not a line officer," said Gerber. "We'll have to watch them to make sure they don't get themselves killed."

Bocker picked up his radio and said, "Aye aye, Captain."

THREE HOURS LATER, Bocker was on the berm again. A huge part of the paddies surrounding the camp had been scooped up and dumped on the perimeter, creating the barricade Gerber had ordered. A new dike, two feet high, had been erected at the edge of the field to hold the paddy water out, so that the moat Gerber had talked about was now a giant red scar of drying, stinking mud. It was the perfect place to land the ten inbound helicopters carrying Sergeant David Santini and the strike company from the Moc Hoa Mike Force.

Bocker ran out and told the bulldozer driver that the choppers were coming in and would be landing there. The man shrugged, took a long pull at the canteen sitting next to him and drove off. He shut down the bulldozer and dropped to the ground, sitting in the shade that it created now that the morning mist had burned off.

The silence was deafening. It was suddenly so quiet that Bocker wondered if he might have gone deaf. Then in the distance came the faint pop of more rotors and the radio crackled to life again.

Cursing the noise, Bocker popped a smoke, listened as the lead pilot identified the color and set up his approach. The Hueys came in hot, flared as if someone had given a command and then settled to the ground. As their skids touched down, the men of the strike company poured from the cargo compartments.

They all moved ten or twelve feet from the choppers and crouched, their eyes closed. The lead chopper came to a hover, turned so that the aircraft commander could see the whole flight and then straightened out again. He lifted off and the rest of the helicopters joined him, climbing out.

As soon as the helicopters were gone and it was silent around the hamlet again, Santini shouted a command at the strikers, getting them all to their feet. They formed a ragged line, did a right face and began walking toward the entrance of the hamlet. Bocker stood watching the show, wondering if he should alert Gerber.

Gerber appeared then and waited until Santini got close. "Welcome aboard, Sergeant."

Santini nodded. "We've arrived. Where do you want us?"

A series of bunkers around the perimeter of the hamlet had been blown up by the Vietcong. A little work and they would make good quarters for the strikers, more comfortable than some of the hootches. It would also keep them on the line where they would be needed if the attack came.

"Get with Sully Smith. He'll help you get the men situated. They'll have to rebuild the bunkers, but that shouldn't be a difficult task."

"Yes, sir."

Gerber turned and said, "Sully's the one in jungle fatigues with the guy who looks like he belongs in the World."

Santini nodded. "Got it." He waved a hand in the air and the strikers began moving into the hamlet.

"You think this is a good idea?" Bocker asked.

"What in the hell could be wrong with it? We've got a strike company in here that we can trust."

"Yes, sir," said Bocker, "but they're not Vietnamese. They're Montagnards who hate the Vietnamese. We could have some trouble with the locals."

"Christ!" Gerber said, "I hadn't thought about that. I was only interested in getting a strike company in here I could trust. Guess it means we'll just have to work that much harder."

"Yes, sir," said Bocker.

"Now the only thing you've got to worry about is getting the supply choppers in here this afternoon and getting the equipment put down where we don't have to move it too far."

"I'd thought of that," Bocker said.

"If we can survive tonight, we should be in very good shape. It all depends on what the VC are planning. I wish I had some clue about that."

SERGEANT FETTERMAN STOOD at the edge of what was a small clearing in the tree line, and looked at the evidence scattered on the ground in front of him. It wasn't the sanitary base camp that had been abandoned by the Vietcong, but a camp that had been evacuated quickly. The enemy usually cleaned up after themselves, leaving nothing of value for the Americans to find, but that wasn't the case here. From the smoking cooking fires and the pots left hanging over them, he knew that the Vietcong had fled quickly.

The fires were interesting. They had a series of broad palm leaves over them that dissipated the smoke so that three or four feet above the ground, it was invisible. There were twelve such fires, set in holes so that the light couldn't be seen. It allowed the enemy to build fires close to American camps without giving the Americans clues about them.

There were some rucksacks, pouches holding magazines for AK-47s, canteens, sandals, papers, parts of uniforms and a hundred other things. The camp was only fifty yards from where the mortar tube had been the night before.

Looking at the camp and the trees, Fetterman was suddenly worried. The camp was big enough for a reinforced company. Two or three hundred men had been there. Since they hadn't stood and fought, it meant that the enemy was planning something else. Fetterman's squad would have been easily chopped up by them if they had fought.

One of the grunts broke from cover and entered the camp, searching for souvenirs. Fetterman stopped him with a single, harsh word. Then he said to Warren, "We've got to get out of here. We make contact and we're going to get killed."

Warren could see the evidence for himself. He snapped a finger and pointed to the rear. One of his men slipped away, taking the point. Without a word, the patrol pivoted, formed and began working its way back toward the hamlet.

As the squad disappeared, Fetterman slipped into the rearguard position. He let the patrol get far ahead of him, staying back, off the trail, trying to find the enemy. He was sure they had to be watching. The camp had been abandoned too quickly. Someone had to have alerted the Vietcong about the approaching Americans.

It didn't make a great deal of sense. Almost anyone who saw the camp would know that a large group of VC had been there. Maybe they assumed that the Americans would be dumb enough to believe the VC were afraid of them. But that wasn't what it meant.

Fetterman slipped from the path and dropped to one knee. He could hear the occasional mistake made by the grunts: a leafy branch against the cloth of a uniform, a foot snapping a twig.

Then from the opposite direction came a similar sound. He knew the VC were working their way back to their camp. They'd probably clean the site, now that it had been found by the Americans, and quietly move it somewhere else. Somewhere not too far away.

Fetterman waited a moment longer and saw a flash of dark clothing against the deep green background of the jungle. The Vietcong were putting out their guards in case the Americans returned before they could get out.

The man knelt near the trunk of a huge tree. Through gaps in the vegetation, Fetterman could see part of his face, his

shoulder and a small portion of his rifle. He was watching the
jungle in front of him, searching for the enemy. Fetterman
thought about sneaking up and killing him, but could see no
point. Let the man live a while longer.

Fetterman moved to the rear, sliding through the jungle
like an evening breeze. He was a ghost who disturbed nothing, an apparition. He kept his eyes moving and his ears
open. He was aware of the animals, the lizards and a single,
brightly colored snake. He didn't bother any of them. He
avoided them and caught the rear of the patrol as it reached
the edge of the trees.

Warren halted the men. As Fetterman approached, he
asked, "What'd you see?"

Fetterman held up a hand to silence the other sergeant.
Then when he was close, he leaned over so that his lips were
only inches from Warren's ear. "They came back within
minutes of our leaving. They're cleaning up and getting
out."

"Maybe we should call in artillery on them."

"I thought of that," said Fetterman, "but I'm not sure it's
a good idea."

"Why?"

"Tells them we know they're here. Might force their hand.
If they believe we don't know about them, then they might
hold off on the attack."

Warren snapped his head around so that he was looking at
Fetterman. Their noses were an inch apart. He was aware of
Fetterman in a way that he was rarely aware of people.

"What attack are you talking about?"

"That's the point of this drill," Fetterman said. "Enemy
knows we're here, and he's getting ready to hit the hamlet
again. Drive us all out."

"How does he know we're here?"

"Christ, man, we didn't exactly sneak in. I arrived in a chopper. You heard the other choppers coming in and flying out. Charlie knows what that means and he's getting ready to hit us and drive us out."

"Then what do we do?"

"We get back to the hamlet and warn the captain about what we've found. We prepare for the attack and hope it doesn't come tonight because we won't be ready for it."

AFTER SHE HAD TALKED to Gerber, drunk her morning coffee with him, Robin went off to work on her story. It was reminiscent of the times at the old Triple Nickel—Gerber and the men fighting the war while she attempted to report it. They'd developed a good relationship about that. She understood their needs and they understood hers. She wouldn't report on anything that would harm them and they, therefore, concealed nothing from her. Although she didn't know it, she was one of the few reporters who had such a relationship. Things like that hadn't existed since World War II.

Now, with more soldiers arriving at the hamlet, the first group brought on a Chinook and the second in Hueys, she noticed that the villagers were even more wary. She still hadn't been able to talk to them, but she had seen their reactions. At first, as more Americans arrived, there was apprehension. But when the strikers landed, there was fear.

Morrow stayed near the center of the hamlet, where the remains of the arms locker stood. She sat there, a camera in one hand, and watched the reaction to the strikers. If she had ever seen fear on the faces of people, she was seeing it now. The men and women were frightened. They stayed in the ruins of their hootches, peeking out at the intruders and refusing to come out, even when offered food and medicine. They didn't look like the people of World War II, who had swarmed into the streets to greet the liberators. They looked like the French as the Nazis marched into Paris.

She took pictures of the helicopters landing. She had pictures of the Chinook with the bulldozer dangling under it. She took more pictures as the flight of ten choppers came in. First just a series of specks in the distance, then obviously a flight, and finally as they approached the ground she shot a sequence of the combat assault.

Then she turned her camera on the Vietnamese in the village. At first they were curious about the strikers and then frightened. They hid from the newcomers, refusing to come out or acknowledge them.

Finally she hopped off the wall where she sat, put her camera in the bag and began to wander through the hamlet. There was activity around her: the strikers filtering into the bunker line and dropping into the bunkers, the Green Berets working with them and the Navy men outside to strengthen the defensive perimeter.

She watched the men as they rebuilt the hamlet. The officers directed the work. She noticed that no one consulted the Vietnamese. They just went about it, doing what they had to do to make the hamlet more defensible. No consideration was given to the Vietnamese and their wishes.

She took pictures of the men working with the bulldozer and then noticed something else. It was midmorning, the sun was baking the fields, but no one was working there. The Vietnamese didn't even attempt to enter the fields. They stayed hidden, sneaking peeks at the activity.

Morrow put the camera back in her bag and headed through the hamlet again. She found Gerber holding a small map and pointing at the tree line that was the closest. Bocker was there, nodding. As she approached, Bocker trotted off.

"Hey, Mack," she said.

Gerber turned. "What?"

"You notice anything about these people?"

"You mean other than the fact there is no one here of military age? They're either old or young, but no one in between."

"Yeah, other than that. No one's in the fields. They haven't come out of hiding."

Gerber rolled up his map, looking like the foreman at a construction site. If it hadn't been for the military equipment and the weapons, she could have almost believed that.

"Now that you mention it."

"Look, I tried to talk to some of the people this morning, but they claimed they couldn't speak English."

"So what do you want me to do about it?"

"Well, Sergeant Fetterman speaks some Vietnamese. I thought maybe I could use him to interpret for me."

Gerber wiped the sweat from his face and glanced up at the burning sun. Somehow, out here, the sun didn't seem quite as bad as it did in the city. Maybe it was all the concrete and stone that absorbed the heat. The open fields, the water and the jungle helped to keep the heat down.

To Morrow, he said, "Tony has no time for this. He has duties to perform."

"Mack, you should know me well enough by now not to try and steer me away from whatever's happening."

"I'm doing no such thing. Just what are you looking for, Robin? What do you think is happening?"

She shrugged. "I can't really pin it down. But I will get at it. Something isn't ringing true."

Gerber was going to tell her that he didn't have the time to waste on her suspicions, especially when she couldn't put them into words. Then he thought about it, and realized that she was asking a question that should be asked. He had never gone into a village or hamlet where the people acted so strange. He'd entered a few where it was obvious that Americans were hated, and he'd entered more where it was obvious that Americans were liked. Maybe they were liked only for the food and money and cigarettes they carried, but they weren't ignored. But here everyone stayed away from the soldiers as if staying away would somehow save the people. Maybe the reason was that the Vietcong were still near, and that earlier the Americans had pulled out. There just weren't any easy answers for all the questions that he had.

"How do you feel about finding out some things for me?" asked Gerber.

"You want me to become a pawn of the military-industrial complex that is going to destroy the free world?"

"No, I want you to do exactly what you want to do. Find out what's going on here."

"Then you'll let Tony help me when he gets back?"

"Santini speaks some Vietnamese and might be able to help. You know Santini, don't you?"

"Sure. I've seen him a couple of times."

Gerber started to walk toward the bunker line. "He's got to get his people working, but afterward he can probably break loose to help you."

Morrow fell in beside Gerber. "You know what it is that's going on, don't you, Mack? I think *I've* got it figured out."

Gerber stopped and stared at her. "Then you don't really want to talk to the people?"

"No, I have to. Maybe I should say I have a theory, but that's all it is. I want these people to tell me without me prompting them."

They found Santini at one corner of the hamlet, working to site a Browning M-2 .50-caliber machine gun so that it could be used against a force attacking from either of two directions. Beside it would be M-60s for support and a couple of grenadiers to lob M-79 rounds into the attacking VC—

if they attacked. It would make that portion of the bunker line difficult to penetrate.

"Sergeant Santini. Do you know Miss Morrow?"

Santini turned and looked at Gerber and Morrow. He wore a tailored uniform of tiger stripes that matched those worn by the strike force. It was soaked with sweat. He didn't have a rucksack and wore only a pistol belt that held a single canteen. He knew his group wouldn't be too far from a base for resupply. Santini looked a great deal like Fetterman—small and dark and tough. He was younger than the master sergeant, this being his first war, but no less deadly.

"Yes, sir. Know her well."

"Good," Gerber said. "I want you to work with her and interpret for her. She's going to quiz the Vietnamese and find out a few things that we all need to know."

"I'm just getting started here, sir."

"I know. Sergeant Smith can fill in for you. Besides, it looks like your men have got a good idea of what they're doing. This is information that we need."

Santini sighed and then stepped to the side where he'd set his weapon and pack. "I'm ready when she is."

"Get with it," said Gerber, "and let me know what you find out."

He didn't know that the worst news was yet to come.

10

MACV HEADQUARTERS
SAIGON

Collins sat looking at the report for five minutes, wondering if it was important enough to bother the general about. It wasn't much, really, just an update by the Air Force. It covered the border region near Duc Bang and the hundreds of electronic sensors that had been planted along the Cambodian border and the Ho Chi Minh Trail. Those sensors, devices thrown from aircraft, picked up the vibrations of people moving along the trail or across the border, and recorded the passage of people by their body heat, or used an electronic beam to detect enemy movements. The sophisticated electronics provided good information that was too often ignored by the brass and the intelligence community.

Now Collins had a report that a fairly large group of people was moving from Cambodia, more or less in the direction of Duc Bang. The numbers were rough, but the indications were that a battalion was on the move. Four or five hundred men, crossing the border but not moving far beyond it.

Collins finally closed the folder and left his office, a cubicle on the corridor. He walked down the hall and entered

Padgett's office. Padgett's Vietnamese secretary stood when he entered, smiled at him broadly and waited for him to speak first.

"Need to see the general," he said.

"General busy."

Collins had to grin because that was what she said to everyone who requested to see the general.

"It's really quite important and I won't take up much of his time."

"I see."

She left her position behind the desk. She wasn't wearing her usual *ao dai*. She was dressed in a short skirt, white blouse and knee-high boots. Her long black hair hung free to the waist. She looked as if she had just left a nightclub in the World. Collins understood exactly why she was employed and also understood that she could type, too.

She reappeared and said, "General see you."

"Thanks." He walked past her and thought about asking her if she'd like to have a drink at the club that evening. But he didn't. The power of the general frightened him. He didn't want to end up humping the boonies with the Vietnamese shooting at him.

As he entered the office, Padgett asked, "What do you have today?"

Collins crossed the floor and handed the report to Padgett, then slipped into the chair opposite the desk without being invited.

Padgett glanced through the report, then looked at Collins. "Why don't you summarize this for me."

"Yes, General. It says that using our electronic detection methods and sensors planted along the Cambodia border, we've detected four or five hundred men crossing, all in the vicinity of Duc Bang."

"And this means?"

"Indications are those men are staying in that general area. I believe it suggests that an attack on Duc Bang is being planned."

"You realize such an attack has already taken place and that the enemy then withdrew?"

"Yes, sir. I understand that. I think the Vietcong were disappointed that the only defenders of Duc Bang were the Ruff-Puffs who lived there."

Padgett set the report on his desk. "You want to elaborate?"

Collins rubbed his face as if thinking quickly. "I've always been bothered by that attack. The Vietcong seemed almost humane in the assault. Granted, they shot the men who opposed them and took off with the young men and women of military age, but there wasn't the widespread destruction that I'd expect. They left most of the people alive."

"They blew up every bunker and burned the hootches."

"In a very calculated way. A little work and the bunkers are repaired. A little concrete and a few cinder blocks and the school and the dispensary can be rebuilt. There's an incentive for us to return because the work we did there hasn't all been eliminated by them."

"You're driving at something here."

"Of course, General. I think we're being set up. I think the Vietcong did what they did with an eye to drawing us back. Once we've put some people into Duc Bang, they plan to overrun it and destroy everything."

"Now why in the hell would they do that?"

"An object lesson. They blow in, kill those who are obviously against them, the armed men, but leave everyone else alive. They blow up the bunkers and burn the hootches to teach everyone a lesson. Then they leave. The Americans return and are welcomed, so the Vietcong attack again, killing everyone in sight."

Padgett touched the folder in front of him. "All that from this report?"

"And a little guesswork. It's the only thing that makes sense. The Vietcong aren't known for their mercy. I wondered why they didn't just shoot everyone and burn the hamlet to the ground to hide the atrocity, and then I realized it would be no real victory. So they'd murdered a bunch of farmers. Where's the glory?"

"So you're saying they'll let us establish a foothold there and then strike with a vengeance."

"Yes, sir. Either tonight or tomorrow night. They won't wait long. I think we'd better alert the men out there."

Padgett stood and walked to his window. He glanced out at the open ground that sloped gently down to a parking lot filled with jeeps, trucks and a few staff cars. An MP guarded them from a little hut at the corner.

He turned and faced Collins. "I'm sure Captain Gerber is aware of his vulnerable position out there."

"Then we're not going to alert him?"

"Oh, hell no. We'll tell him we believe there's an enemy battalion in the area that might be massing for an assault. We'll also lay on some artillery support, fighter support and arrange for reinforcements. How many men does Gerber have there now?"

"Last time I checked, the infantry platoon that swept through yesterday was still there. He's got some Seabees, five or six Special Forces men and a company of strikers, about ninety men from Moc Hoa."

"Then there really isn't much for us to do here, but watch the situation."

"No, General, I guess not. I just thought I'd better advise you of the situation."

"Thank you, Captain."

FETTERMAN HELD the patrol at the edge of the tree line for twenty minutes, watching and listening. The VC never bothered to come close to them, and in fact, seemed to be uninterested in them. He guessed that the VC outnumbered him five or six to one, the kind of odds they liked. Before they initiated an attack, they liked to be certain they could win the fight. Jumping a small patrol with a company was exactly the kind of thing the VC liked the best. Still they didn't show up.

From his vantage point, Fetterman could monitor the activity in Duc Bang. He was searching for weaknesses in the defenses and saw a dozen of them. Holes in the berm, bunkers that hadn't been repaired and high ground in the center of the hamlet so that anyone standing there would be an easy target for a sniper in the trees. He could see the people in the hamlet.

"Shitty location, militarily, for a camp," he mumbled.

Warren, who was crouched near him, said, "Hey, we didn't pick it."

Fetterman turned and said, "I wonder who did. The Vietcong? An attack on it would be easy to organize."

"Then we must strengthen that part of the perimeter," said Warren.

"We ought to erect a wall through the center so the enemy won't be able to snipe easily."

"Let's get out of here," said Warren.

Fetterman nodded. "You take your patrol and head on out. I'll stay here with Sergeant Tyme for a rear guard."

Warren got to his feet and touched one man on the shoulder. That soldier moved to the very edge of the tree line. Warren quietly alerted the rest of his men, though with the noise from the bulldozer drifting to them, it would be difficult to give away their position. When they were ready, Warren glanced to the rear where Fetterman and Tyme waited in case the VC decided to follow.

Warren then signaled to the point man who left the tree line. He walked along on a rice paddy dike, turned onto another and began to work his way toward the hamlet. He walked slowly, his eyes on the dike in front of him, searching for a booby trap or trip wire. He also watched the ground around him, and searched the hamlet in front of him. His head seemed to be on a swivel as he tried to take everything in as he moved.

The patrol was strung out behind him, using the dikes that he had used, each man searching the ground for a booby trap. One, two, a half dozen men might step over the booby trap so that every man had to search for them. It was the one thing that made patrols the constant strain they were. There was always the threat of an enemy ambush, but there were a dozen clues to look for. There was a threat of rats and snakes and even tigers, but those were no worse than the threats of a hike through Yellowstone.

But the booby traps were something to be feared. The clue could be so small that it would be impossible to see. The VC were known to bury a single rifle round with a nail against the primer that would fire when someone stepped on it. The bullet would penetrate the foot and sometimes travel up the leg, ripping muscle and blood vessels and shattering bone. With bad luck it could sever the femoral artery, killing a man in seconds.

So they moved slowly, no longer worried about the company of VC behind them because Fetterman and Tyme were guarding them. If the VC tried to attack, Fetterman and Tyme would provide some warning.

And then they were only a few yards from the berm. There were soldiers there, watching them. The Seabees ignored them, keeping the bulldozer running, the noise from the diesel engine overwhelming all other sound.

As they reached the berm, Warren turned and saw Fetterman and Tyme coming at them. Neither man looked worried or in a hurry. They followed the path that the patrol had taken.

Fetterman reached the hamlet finally. "Let's go find the captain."

Warren nodded but hesitated. "I should report to Lieutenant Helmsman."

"We'll get to him," said Fetterman, "but we've got to brief the captain first."

"You're the boss," Warren said.

Fetterman turned to Tyme. "Justin, get these guys organized. A break and then find something for them to do."

"Sure, Tony."

The two sergeants headed toward the center of the hamlet. They spotted Gerber near the arms locker, talking to one of the Seabees. As soon as the Navy man moved away, Fetterman approached and said, "Got a problem, Captain."

Gerber turned and shook his head. "That's all we need. Another problem. What'd you find?"

Fetterman stepped closer and lowered his voice. "I think there's a big VC force hidden around here, just waiting for a chance to hit us."

"How many?"

"I don't know for sure. We found evidence of a company-size force. But we didn't search very far. Could be another company or two in there."

"Damn!" said Gerber. "I don't see how we can be ready for them tonight."

"Yes, sir," said Fetterman. "I think we'd better get ready because I don't think they're going to wait very long."

"No," said Gerber, "I don't suppose they will."

MORROW AND SANTINI crouched in the shade of one of the
hootches and stared at the people inside. Both were sitting
on their heels, as the Vietnamese did. It was an uncomfortable position that put a strain on the muscles of the thighs.
The Vietnamese could crouch that way for hours. Morrow
wasn't sure how long she could do it.

The three women and two men in the wrecked hootch had
been talking among themselves until Morrow and Santini
arrived. Then they had fallen silent and refused to talk.

"What were they saying?" Morrow asked.

"Not much," said Santini. "They were talking fast.
Something about the soldiers, but I couldn't catch it all. I'm
not sure if they were talking about us, or the VC."

Morrow sat there watching them for a moment and then
said, "Why don't you ask them what happened here?"

"We know what happened," said Santini.

"Sure, but it's a way to get things started. Besides, we
don't know the details."

Santini studied the ground in front of him. He could smell
the odor of burned wood and burned flesh. A whiff of open
sewer came from somewhere, carried on a light breeze. And
there was the odor of unwashed bodies. The people in the
hootch hadn't bothered with bathing since the attack by the
VC.

Finally he looked up, stared at one of the old men until the
man glanced at him. The man wore black pajamas and a
coolie hat. He had a long mustache and a gray beard. When
he looked up, Santini asked in Vietnamese, "What did the
Vietcong do in the hamlet?"

There was no response.

Santini shot a glance at Morrow and asked, "VC come in
the night and they kill?"

Again, no one spoke. They all watched Santini now, as if
surprised that he could speak Vietnamese.

"I don't know, Robin," he said. "I don't think these people are going to talk."

"Then ask them what they're afraid of. Find out where all the young people are. Do something."

Santini sat quietly, forming the questions. He pointed at the oldest man. "Why are you afraid?"

For a moment it seemed that no one was going to speak again. Then the old man said simply, "You."

"Us? You're afraid of us?" Morrow touched her chest. "But why?"

"Because if you weren't here, the VC would not be here," replied the old man.

"What did he say?" asked Morrow.

"He said they were afraid of us. Said that we're the reason that the VC are here."

"But we're here to protect them and help them," said Morrow.

"Yes, ma'am," Santini responded. "That's the official line from Saigon."

Morrow looked surprised. "Now what in the hell do you mean by that?"

"Nothing," said Santini.

"Tell them we're here to repair their hamlet so that it will be a good place to live."

Santini translated the statement, but none of the Vietnamese responded to it.

"What's going on?" asked Morrow.

"I've been at this a long time," said Santini. "I've seen frightened people and these people are frightened. I think they're afraid of everyone. They have no control over their lives. We come in and start building things. We leave and the Vietcong shows up."

"That your theory?" Morrow asked.

"Look around you," said Santini. "I've worked with a lot of the Vietnamese. You see them rushing out to help us rebuild their hamlet? Hell, do you see us doing them any good right now?"

"What do you mean?"

"We come in here to help them, but we're rebuilding the bunkers and the defensive perimeter first."

Morrow wiped the sweat from her face. "But that has to be done first."

"Yes, ma'am, from a military standpoint it does. But ask yourself what this strategic hamlet concept is all about. And ask yourself about the results of the concept."

"I don't understand."

Santini turned, spoke quickly to the Vietnamese and then stood. He shaded his face with a hand to his eyes and said, "You don't need to talk to the people."

"Sure I do," said Morrow. "I need to interview them so I can understand what's happening here."

Santini held out a hand and helped her to her feet. "You don't have to talk to them because their actions speak volumes about what's going on here."

Morrow followed Santini's gaze. She saw the bulldozer creating a chest-high barrier around the hamlet. There were men working in the bunkers, recreating them by using the sandbags and beams that hadn't been destroyed. A group of Americans were working around the arms locker, separating the broken cinder blocks from those that could be used again. Equipment was stacked near the locker. A third group sat to one side, smoking cigarettes and drinking from their canteens. It was the only place where the Vietnamese and the Americans mixed. A few old men were begging for cigarettes.

Morrow noticed that all the construction was on the military structures. The school, the dispensary and the hootches

were all being ignored. The standing water at the low spots
was ignored, although the pools smelled like a sewer and were
a breeding ground for mosquitoes. Beyond that were the
open, empty fields. By this time of the day, the paddies
should have been swarming with workers, but the Vietnamese stayed inside the hamlet, refusing to venture out.

"They don't have to farm anymore," said Santini. "This
afternoon, when the choppers bring in the building materials, they'll bring in rice. Bags of it."

"Is there something going on here that I don't know
about?" asked Morrow.

"Nothing that I'd care to speculate about. But you see
what's happening. What does it mean to you?"

"Mack said that we've come in to help the people defend
themselves."

"Captain Gerber is a good man," said Santini. "He looks
around here and sees what has to be done. He'll get it done,
but in the end, what good will it do?"

"Sergeant," Morrow said, "you're not making yourself
clear at all."

"This off the record?"

"Christ, I don't know what you're talking about."

"I just don't want to open the newspaper and see myself
quoted. I like my job, and the military can make life miserable for the man who seems to be a renegade."

"If you have something to say, you can say it. I won't go
spreading your name all over the newspapers."

Santini nodded and started to walk away. He stopped short
and took out his canteen. He drank deeply and then poured
a little water in the palm of his hand. He rubbed it on the back
of his neck.

"I think we've pretty well seen exactly how effective the
strategic hamlet concept is going to be."

"You mean because of Tet?"

"Think about it. We abandoned the hamlets, moving our soldiers from them to meet the needs of the Army during Tet. Our troops went off to fight elsewhere. Now, the strategic hamlets were designed so that the locals could take care of themselves when the soldiers left. The assumption is that the Americans will leave someday. We don't want to be in Vietnam forever, you know."

"Makes sense."

"So, we create the strategic hamlet, but long before we blast out of here, we have a chance to test the concept. We're so busy with the fight in the cities that we can't worry about a couple of little hamlets near the border. Hamlets that are supposed to be able to defend themselves."

Morrow began to nod. "I see what you're saying. The concept was tested and failed. Without the Americans here, the enemy just walked in and did whatever they wanted."

"And these people know it, too. Without us to back them up, they're going to switch to the Communists, because if they don't, they'll die. Hell, right now, they're afraid to be seen cooperating. This whole thing has failed already."

Morrow understood exactly. It was what had been bothering her since she'd arrived the day before. She just hadn't been able to put it into words.

"We've got to do something about it," she said with sudden conviction.

"What?" asked Santini.

It was then that she understood the problem.

11

MACV HEADQUARTERS
SAIGON

Padgett was sitting at his desk, the air conditioner blowing cold air at him as he smoked his pipe. A cloud of blue circled his head and drifted toward the door on the artificial breeze created by the air-conditioning. When there was a light tapping on the door, Padgett grinned and shouted, "Come."

Collins entered, wearing fresh jungle fatigues. His uniform had been heavily starched, and looked crisp and clean and perfect. The sleeves were rolled up halfway between the elbow and the shoulder, just as regulations dictated. The subdued insignia sewn to his collar and above his pockets contained no cables. There was nothing in any of the pockets to break the lines of the uniform. He had shaved recently and had combed his short-cropped hair.

"Excuse me, General," he said, "but it's almost time for your briefing with the congressional delegation."

Padgett looked at his watch. "We've what, five, ten minutes?"

"Ten minutes."

"Then sit," said Padgett, gesturing at the chair.

"I'll stand, sir, if you don't mind. I don't want to wrinkle my uniform."

Padgett nodded. "How do I look?"

"Fine, General. Just fine."

Padgett walked across to the bookcase, touched the upper corner of a book and let it fold out of the way. Bending down, he recovered the hidden bottle of Scotch and then straightened.

"Can I interest you in a touch of the wet stuff?" he asked.

"No, sir," said Collins. "I'm . . . I . . ."

"Don't tell me you're worried about these congressmen. Hell, man, they're not that smart. Got themselves a junket to Vietnam, but I'll bet you cash money they'll be stopping in Hong Kong, Japan, Hawaii, and anywhere else they can think of. This is merely their excuse to be in this part of the world."

"If you think no one will notice . . ."

"Hell, what are they going to do? Send you to Vietnam as punishment?"

Collins laughed. "I thought only the enlisted men talked that way."

"I may be a general, but I know what's going on. If I didn't, I wouldn't be much of a general." He pulled a couple of glasses out of a desk drawer and set them on his desk. He removed the stopper from the bottle and dumped a couple of fingers of alcohol into the glasses. After he set the bottle down, he handed a glass to Collins.

"Cheers," he said, and drained his glass. He breathed out and shuddered instinctively, making a face. "Now I'm ready to face the congressional delegation."

Collins swallowed the liquor quickly and set the glass on the desk, then walked to the door and opened it. "They're in the commander's conference room."

"Of course," Padgett said. "Wouldn't want our elected officials to have to put up with anything less than the best."

As they passed through the outer office, Padgett nodded to the Vietnamese woman. "I'll be gone for about an hour or so. Take messages for me."

"Yes, General," she said.

The two men hurried down the hallway until they came to the door of the conference room. Padgett tugged at his jungle jacket, ran a hand through his hair, then opened the door. He nodded at the two men in the outer office.

"I'm expected," said Padgett.

"Yes, General," a lieutenant responded. "Go right in."

The conference room was almost the size of a gymnasium. A massive mahogany table was set in the center and surrounded by judge's chairs. There were several silver tea services spaced around it so that no one would have to reach very far for a drink of water. A huge screen occupied one end. A giant American flag stood in one corner and a Vietnamese flag in the other. There was a thick carpet on the floor, paneling on the walls, and a few watercolors depicting local scenes. The lighting was subdued.

Twelve enlisted men, wearing khaki uniforms, were stationed around the room. They were aides assigned to the congressmen.

Padgett stopped just inside the door and waited. General Creighton Abrams sat at the head of the table, talking quietly to one of the congressional representatives, a solidly built man with sparse hair and a bad attitude. He mopped his face with a handkerchief.

Abrams noticed Padgett and waved him forward. "Right on time, General. We're ready for you now."

Padgett moved to the lectern standing near the screen and said, "Thank you, General. Gentleman, today I want to discuss the strategic hamlet concept and how it relates to our vision of a reduction of American support in the war.''

He wished he'd thought of putting together a slide briefing. That was becoming the way to do it in the military. No longer were the top officers willing to let a man brief from a map. Now they wanted pictures of everything, a slide show, no matter how marginally related to the subject.

He glanced at his audience. Senators and representatives and their assistants, without wives or female congressional watchdogs. Most wore light suits, shirts and ties. Not exactly the best dress for the tropics, but then, they had an image to maintain. He wondered how much he could ask for the use of his secretary. He'd bet that some of the men would give him practically anything for a shot at her.

He turned his attention back to the topic at hand—the strategic hamlets, describing how a similar program had been used by the British in Malaysia. He explained its use and history in Vietnam and pointed out that it had met with only limited success until now. During Tet, the American command had determined that American troops could be better used elsewhere. But the concept was good. Give the people the means to defend themselves from the Communists and there'd be a reduction in the effectiveness of the Vietcong.

"This is a concept whose time has come," Padgett said, winding up. "We can reduce the amount of territory we must cover with the use of the strategic hamlets."

"Question, General," said one of the congressmen. "What is the attitude of the local population?"

Padgett nodded once and stared at the ceiling as if formulating an answer. He'd been ready for the question and had prepared an answer for it before he'd walked into the room.

"There's a great deal of local support for the program. What we're doing is allowing the farmer to do what he wants to do, that is, farm his land. Now he doesn't have to worry about the Vietcong terrorists attacking his village, stealing his food and killing his family. For this, all we ask is that he take a hand in the defense of the village if the enemy decides to attack.''

"So how does this free our men?"

"Once we have the people trained, we pull our men out. It's true that we must keep a reaction team ready, but instead of tying our men down to a single hamlet, we have them available to help half a dozen. Reduces our troop requirement.''

"I don't see how this lets us bring our boys home," said another man.

"Well, sir. If we have five hamlets with troops in each of them, say one hundred men in each, we have five hundred soldiers in the field. Now, under the strategic hamlet concept, the locals take some of the responsibility for their own defense and we provide a reaction force of say, one hundred men. The other four hundred can go home."

"But we still have one hundred men in the field."

"At the present time, yes, sir. But what we think will happen is the Vietcong will find no support in the region where those five hamlets are. They'll pull their soldiers out, sending them elsewhere and then our one hundred men will be free to leave. Merely a question of organizing the locals, training them and letting them drive the VC from their homes through a lack of support."

"Speaking of support," said the congressman, "are you sure that we have it?"

Padgett clasped his hands together and leaned his elbows on the lectern. "Of course. What we're doing is helping these people with more than defense. We rebuild the area, giving them stronger, better homes. We construct sanitation facilities, schools, dispensaries and other community buildings.

While the people are working with us on that, we supply food for them. We teach them everything they need to survive in this environment. There is no one who complains about this."

Before Padgett or anyone else could say anything more, Abrams said, "Thank you, General. A most thorough account of the concept."

Padgett said, "Thank you, General. Gentlemen. If there are additional questions, I'll be in my office for your convenience."

He left then. In the hallway, Collins asked, "How do you think it went?"

"Just fine. They heard what they wanted to hear. We're making progress in the war and finding ways to reduce our involvement. Everyone's happy."

"Good," said Collins.

"Very good," agreed Padgett.

FETTERMAN SAT ON A WALL of sandbags watching the activity around him. The Seabees had returned to their bulldozer and were trying to create a moat and a berm. The strikers were busy building bunkers. The Americans were sitting around acting as if they were on guard duty.

He noticed two Vietnamese standing near what had been the arms locker. The old man was clutching a bundle in his arms and the woman held a small black pot. They were looking at the remains of a mud hootch. There wasn't much left of it. The walls had collapsed and the roof had burned, leaving black ash in the center. Fetterman knew they were looking at what was left of their home and the few things they had owned.

The man glanced around at all the activity. He touched the woman on the shoulder, and together they turned and walked toward the rear of the hamlet, away from the area where the bulldozer worked or the Americans stood guard. They moved from hootch to hootch, stopping at each and speaking to the people in it. Finally they reached the berm, hesitated and then were over it, walking into the fields.

Getting out, thought Fetterman. They had nothing left and they were getting out. They said goodbye to their friends before they left.

He stood up, wondering if he should mention what he'd seen to anyone. Why should he? The people were free to go if they wanted. It wasn't as if they were ARVN or members of a strike force. They were villagers who could move to another hamlet if they wanted.

But as he stood there, he saw another family leave. The ritual was almost the same. They studied the remains of what had been their home, carried everything they owned and said goodbye to everyone they knew. Finally they sneaked out the back, away from the activity of the reconstruction.

When the family disappeared into the trees west of the camp, Fetterman turned and headed toward Gerber. He found the captain standing at the edge of the hamlet with a map in his hand.

"Sir, I think we've got a problem."

Gerber handed the map to Helmsman and said, "You work out a plan for patrols and I'll look it over."

"Yes, sir."

Gerber pulled Fetterman to the side. "What is it, Tony?"

"I think the villagers are punching out."

"What?"

"They're leaving. Sneaking off with everything they own," said Fetterman.

Gerber glanced over his shoulder, but didn't see anyone. He looked at Fetterman. "What bothers you about it?"

"Here we are rebuilding their homes, and they're getting out. They're not out here helping us. They're hiding from us like we're the Vietcong. They're waiting for the other shoe to fall."

Gerber studied the scene and realized what was wrong with it. None of the villagers were out there helping. None was even watching them. They were all hidden away, in the few standing hootches, out of the sun, waiting for something to happen.

Gerber rubbed his face. He was in a dilemma. Everyone told him how important the hamlet was. It was close to Cambodia. The Vietcong had attacked it. The villagers had resisted, meaning that they supported the Saigon government. But now they hid from the Americans or were sneaking out of the area.

"I see what you mean," Gerber said. "Hadn't paid that much attention to it, but now it seems to scream at me."

"So what are you going to do about it?"

"I think I'm going to find Robin and see what she knows. She's been hanging around with these people all day. Maybe she has a clue."

"Maybe we should just get out, too. Call in the choppers and leave."

"Tony, you know we can't do that. We have our orders and it's to put this place back together."

"Yes, sir."

Gerber watched as Fetterman walked off, heading toward where the Seabees were constructing a berm. He stopped short and crouched, grabbing a handful of the red dust. He let it play through his fingers, blowing away on the light breeze.

"That's one troubled individual," Gerber mumbled, then walked toward the center of the hamlet. He found Morrow and Santini sitting by themselves, talking in low tones. Morrow's jumpsuit with no legs and short sleeves was now wrinkled, stained and dirty. There was soot smeared on her face and she was sweating. She didn't look happy.

Gerber approached and crouched near them. "What's happening here?"

"What do you mean?" asked Morrow.

Gerber waved at the hamlet. "I mean, what's going on? The villagers seem to be slipping out. You know anything about that?"

Morrow nodded. "I've talked with a couple of them. Sergeant Santini translated." She took a deep breath. "Most have decided it's time to go visit relatives elsewhere. They don't want to be caught in the middle of a fight, so they're getting out."

Gerber shot a look at Santini. "There's a fight coming?"

Santini shrugged. "Hell, sir, if I had anything concrete, I would have come to you, but I don't. The impression I get is that these people believe a fight is coming, but only because we're here. If we stayed away, the enemy would stay away and there would be no fight."

"Makes sense," said Gerber.

"You know what these people want?" said Morrow. "They want to be left alone. They just want to grow their food and live their lives without the war."

"There's the rub," said Gerber. "Even if we pulled out, they wouldn't be left alone. Hell, we did, and you can see what happened." He gestured at the burned remains of the hamlet. "The VC came in and burned the place."

"But only because we'd been here. If we hadn't been, then the VC wouldn't have felt the need to punish the villagers."

"Is that how you think of it? As punishment?"

"No," she said, shaking her head. "But that's how *they* think of it. They help you, and the VC punish them. They help the VC, and we punish them."

"Now wait a minute," snapped Gerber. "We don't punish people."

"What I mean is that you, or rather the Americans, see this as a hostile village. Maybe you take a little fire and then artillery is called in to suppress it. Punishment for helping the Vietcong."

"Caught right in the middle," said Santini.

Gerber had to agree. "No matter what they do, they're in trouble with someone."

"Right," said Morrow, "so now they're getting out. Joining family elsewhere."

"The thing is," said Gerber, "that they won't be left alone. Even if we all went home tomorrow, they wouldn't be left alone."

"How do you know?" Morrow asked. She wasn't challenging the statement, but asking for information.

"Because it's the way the Communists work whenever they take over anywhere. They have to separate the educated from the uneducated. The educated tend to ask questions that the Communists don't want to answer. The Communists also arrest anyone who ever helped us in any way."

"But that wouldn't affect the farmers."

"How do you know?" asked Gerber. "Just because they're farmers, it doesn't mean they haven't been educated or worked for the Saigon government. Besides, the Communists almost always collectivize the farms. No one owns the land, the state does. The farmers work it and then the crop is taken to be distributed."

Morrow shook her head and stared at the red dirt. With one finger she traced a pattern in it. "They don't have a chance."

"Well, if we force the Communists out, they do."

"Except that those who helped the VC will be arrested."

"And if they did help the VC, then maybe they should be. But the farmers will be left alone then. No mass executions."

"You don't know about that. For sure," said Morrow.

"No. I didn't read a hell of a lot about the mass grave found at Hue, either. The Communists went in and killed three thousand people. A pretty good indication of what they'll do if they win."

"What a mess," Morrow said.

Fetterman appeared then and said, "Captain, we've got some people coming in."

Gerber stood, glanced at Morrow and Santini. "What people?" he asked.

"Vietnamese. Men and women. About a dozen of them. Told the strikers they lived here and fled when the Vietcong attacked."

"But you don't think so."

Fetterman shrugged. "There's something not right about this."

"Let's go take a look."

Together they moved off, heading toward the side of the hamlet where the bulldozer still worked. Gerber could just see the top of it now. A cloud of black smoke hung around it as the afternoon breeze died, and the air was heavy with humidity. The man driving it had taken off his shirt and his body glistened with sweat. Three others stood around, watching him work.

The newcomers were standing in a line near the arms locker. At their feet were the bundles they had carried. Nine men and three women, all around military age.

Gerber let his eyes sweep the line. All wore black pajamas. A few of the men had on shorts, as did two of the women. They all wore Ho Chi Minh sandals.

"Anyone search the bundles?"

"We made a quick look, but there's nothing in them except some extra clothes and a few personal items."

"No weapons?"

"We didn't find any."

Again Gerber studied the Vietnamese. Unlike most villagers, the people stared back, not dropping their eyes. On a couple of the faces was hatred.

Gerber pulled Fetterman aside and whispered, "If these people are villagers, I'll eat my beret. They're not farmers, and I wouldn't be surprised if a couple of them aren't hardcore regulars."

"Yes, sir," said Fetterman. "So what do we do with them?"

"Christ, that's the question, isn't it? If we send them away, then we're the bad guys. They tell Saigon and we're in the shit. We let them in, and we'll have to watch our backs all the time."

"I can alert the others," said Fetterman.

"Yeah, and have one of our people keep an eye on them at all times, too. And maybe we'd better keep the strikers away from them so we don't end up with a fight."

Gerber looked at his watch and then at the Vietnamese. One of the women had extra-long, black hair that hung below her waist. One of the men looked as if he couldn't be more than fourteen, but all of them looked as if they were the enemy. There didn't seem to be a farmer among them.

As if reading his thoughts, Fetterman said, "Their IDs were all perfect, laminated cards, not the ratty things farmers carry. And none of them have calluses on their hands from working in the fields."

"I think we've had the enemy planted on us," said Gerber.

"Does that mean the attack comes tonight?"

Gerber looked toward the berm, which was now four feet high around most of the village, and then up at the sky where the black clouds were rolling in. The defenses incomplete and the beginnings of a storm, he thought.

"Yeah," he said. "I think we can count on the attack coming tonight."

"Then we'd better get busy," said Fetterman.

"Exactly."

12

THE HAMLET OF DUC BANG, REPUBLIC OF VIETNAM

As soon as the Vietnamese were allowed to enter the hamlet, Gerber began to round up his men. He moved through the hamlet slowly, telling each of them that he wanted to talk to them in a little while, but not to alert anyone else. Afterward, he found Lieutenant Helmsman and Sergeant Warren, and gave them the same message.

They assembled for the informal briefing late in the afternoon, at the southeast corner of the hamlet, away from the droning of the bulldozer, the portion of the bunker line the strikers were rebuilding and most of the hamlet. Gerber wanted privacy, but he also wanted a clear view of the hamlet so no one could sneak up on them. Those people who had entered still bothered him, as did the trickle of Vietnamese who were leaving. It all indicated that something was going on.

Gerber looked at the men seated on the ground facing him. He sat with his back against one of the rebuilt bunkers. The sun dropping toward the horizon was in his face, but Gerber ignored it.

"All right," he said, "I think tonight we're going to get hit and probably hit hard."

He waited for a reaction but there wasn't much of one. Each of the men seemed to have already figured out that the enemy was going to attack.

"There are a number of good reasons for this," said Gerber. He told them about Fetterman's observations in the trees, about the people sneaking out and the VC sneaking in. He pointed out that the earlier attack by the VC had not been much of a success. The enemy had overrun a village defended by a couple of farmers who happened to have World War II vintage weapons. He finished by saying that the indications were that the enemy would hit them that evening, before they had the chance to get everything ready.

"So what are we going to do?" asked Helmsman.

"Organize a few surprises for them. Justin, as soon as we break up here, I want you to find Galvin and begin coordinating the artillery support, both HE for hitting the staging areas and illumins for lighting the assault routes."

"Yes, sir."

"T.J., you'll need to get an aid station set up, probably in what was once the arms locker. That should be the safest place in the hamlet."

Helmsman interrupted. "Captain, I can have my medic assist there."

"Good," Gerber said. "And anyone else with first-aid training, if we don't need him elsewhere."

"Yes, sir."

"Sully, you got any kind of demolitions planned?"

"Well, the supply chopper brought in some claymores and we can get them placed on the outside of the berm. I won't have time to tie them together, so they'll have to be individually detonated. I've a few M-2 bounding mines, but I doubt they'll be useful now. We've picked up some hand grenades and I'll pass those out. I've also got a case of trip flares, but again, I'm not sure how valuable those will be, given the circumstances. We don't have the time to get them placed."

"Galvin, how are we set for commo?"

"Lieutenant Helmsman has his PRC-25. I've got one, too. I've also got a couple of the URC-10s and there are a couple of survival radios but those only work on 242.0. I've talked to the local arty advisories and a couple of the other units, including aviation. Everyone knows we're here. Commo right now is good."

"Santini, what's the bunker line look like?"

"Well, sir, it was a mess. The strikers have spent the day repairing the bunkers as best they can. We don't have all of them covered. They're good fighting positions, but not as solid as bunkers."

"Okay," said Gerber. "Tony, you thought about the distribution of our forces?"

Fetterman nodded. "Yes, sir. I've worked out a plan that will put the American soldiers at the points most likely to be attacked, and then set it up so that the strikers support them. We can shift men from one side of the hamlet to the other, depending on where the VC attack. We'll put our people on the most likely avenues of assault."

"Justin, what about the crew-served weapons?"

"Not much there, sir. The M-2 and the M-60s are all. I'll get with Sergeant Fetterman and we'll figure something out."

"Any questions?" asked Gerber. He looked from face to face. The Special Forces troops knew their jobs and knew what had to be done. Gerber hadn't needed to brief them on it. But he'd wanted everyone to get together just in case someone had an extraordinary idea that could help, and to make sure that nothing was overlooked.

When no one spoke, Gerber said, "We'd better be prepared by dusk. I don't want anyone moving around thirty minutes before sunset. No reason to give some smartass VC an easy target."

"Just like the old Triple Nickel," said Tyme.

"Just like," Gerber agreed. "If there's nothing else, let's get back to work."

The meeting broke up, with the Special Forces men wandering off to complete their tasks. As they did, Lieutenant Helmsman came forward and stood quietly for a moment, as if trying to formulate his question.

In the background, the bulldozer fell silent and Gerber realized that he should have invited the Navy to the meeting. He'd have to talk to their CO in the next few minutes.

He turned his attention back to Helmsman and asked, "You have something on your mind?"

"Well, yes, sir."

Gerber studied the young officer. He wasn't much younger than Jack Bromhead, Gerber's onetime exec, but somehow, this man seemed a lot younger. Maybe it was the lack of training, or the lack of experience in the field. Gerber could see that the man was scared. It was evident in his posture, his downcast eyes and the color of his skin.

"Listen," said Gerber, taking the initiative. "We're in a good position here. The troops are well trained and know what they're doing. Charlie doesn't have the people around to cause us any real trouble. If he does, then we counter with air strikes and artillery, which is being coordinated now."

"Yes, sir, I understand all that."

"But something else is bothering you?"

"Yes, sir." Helmsman looked around as if searching for spies. There was no one in earshot. "I've read about Lang Vei...."

"Yeah," said Gerber. "And?"

"Well, sir, they had tanks. We couldn't stop the tanks."

Gerber grinned. "Don't sweat it. We don't have to worry about tanks. Hell, man, you've been in contact before, you've been mortared, and you lived through it."

"Yes, sir, but they didn't throw a human wave attack at me and they weren't backed by armor. We don't have anything to stop armor."

"That's where you're wrong." Gerber turned and stared out into the rice paddies that surrounded the hamlet. He didn't point, worried about those snipers he'd warned the others about.

"Look at the terrain. Rice paddies full of water. That means the ground is soft. No good for armor."

"But those were Soviet PT-76 amphibious tanks. They can cross rivers."

"But not rice paddies. Not enough water to float them, and the riverbeds are often more solid than the bottom of a rice paddy. Tanks can't maneuver on this terrain. They're the least of our worries."

"And the human wave attacks?"

"Well," Gerber said, "those are a different story. I've seen a few of those and they can get hairy. But then we've good fields of fire all the way to the trees, and with that new berm, it'll be difficult for the enemy to get at us. Fire discipline and coordination will keep the enemy out of the hamlet."

"I don't know, sir. Somehow I feel like William Travis with all the Mexicans in the world outside the Alamo's walls."

"Just remember, if Travis and his men had had automatic weapons, the Mexicans would never have gotten into the fort. In fact, they had a tough time of it anyway. Travis couldn't call on air strikes and artillery, either. He was on his own. We're not."

"Yes, sir."

Gerber turned and looked into the center of the hamlet. "We've a lot of work to do before nightfall. We'd better get to it."

THE NOISE WAS ALMOST unbearable. It came from every corner of the huge room, bouncing off the walls and reverberating in his head. The din from ice in glasses, the clatter of small cocktail plates and silverware, and the chatter were almost too much. Also the smoke from dozens of cigarettes, a few cigars and fewer pipes, made Padgett wish that the party was over.

The general stood in almost the exact center of the room, dressed in a tailored khaki uniform made in Hong Kong that held all his awards and decorations above the left breast pocket. He looked at the pipe in one hand, the tobacco no longer burning, then his gaze shifted to the other hand, which held a glass with a martini and an olive. War might be hell, but the Army managed to get everything necessary for a proper cocktail.

To his left stood Collins, his fatigues no longer quite so fresh looking. There were sweat stains under the arms and down the back, and his hair was no longer perfectly combed. He was not a happy man. Too many careers had been ruined by the wrong word at a cocktail party. He didn't want to see his Army career die an untimely death.

In front of them was a congressman holding a large cigar and a large drink. He was pointing at Padgett with the cigar, unaware that the thing smelled like a burning turd.

"An impressive performance this afternoon," the congressman was saying, his voice booming over the others. "But what do you really think of this strategic hamlet concept? Seems to me that you were handing out a load of crap."

Padgett looked at the woman standing next to the congressman. Twenty years old, maybe twenty-one, with long blond hair and dimples when she smiled. Unfortunately, she was power hungry. She had latched onto a man with power and was now using it. She wasn't interested in the others at the party because they didn't have the power that the congressman had. Still, she was a pretty girl who wore clothing to accent her beauty.

"I believe everything I said," responded Padgett.

"Don't hand me that. I can read you like a book, General, and I can tell that you don't like the idea. What I want to know is why you don't like it."

Padgett sipped his drink and wondered how he could escape without being too obvious. He let his eyes wander over the crowd—the congressmen, the employees of the embassy, the brass from MACV and USARV and the local Vietnamese politicians. A large crowd crammed into the room where the air-conditioning was beginning to fail and the temperature was slowly rising.

But there was no escape. Padgett was trapped. What he had to do was figure out a way to retreat without getting slaughtered.

"I think..." Padgett started. He caught a glimpse of Collins rolling his eyes and looking skyward as if praying. "I think you're misinterpreting my *concern* for a lack of support as *being* a lack of support."

"You care to explain that, General?"

Padgett drained his glass. "Of course. I'm worried about the concept because we aren't doing enough to support it. On paper it's a hell of a good idea, but in the field it stinks. The reason is that we don't commit to it like we should. We put men into the field to train the locals, we arm the locals, but then when there's trouble, or a threat of trouble, we pull out."

"If your plan is effective, then that shouldn't be a problem. You yourself said that the goal is to teach the people to defend themselves."

"Eventually, yes. But we've got to stay long enough to provide that training. We've got to stay long enough to prove that we're not going to desert them when it comes to a showdown."

"Are you suggesting we've done that?" asked the congressman.

"Unfortunately, yes." Padgett was aware of Collins, who looked as if he'd stepped into something warm, soft and smelly. "The circumstances were such that it couldn't be helped. With Tet happening, we needed all our men. But now we've got the opportunity to show the locals that we mean business. We're going to stay and fight with them."

"Again," said the congressman, "we're staying to fight. I thought the point was to get us out of here."

"But first, we have to prove we're willing to fight. Once we've done that and provided the training and equipment, then we'll be able to pull out."

"Bull," said the congressman. He whirled, grabbed the girl's arm and dragged her into the crowd, disappearing quickly.

"Shit, General," said Collins.

"Don't worry, Captain, we can't be killed for spouting the official line."

"Even when everyone sees through it?"

Padgett smiled and clamped his pipe between his teeth. "I remember talking to a CIA type who told me that he always followed his cover story. Even when it was unraveling badly and lay in tatters, he stuck with it. That unnerved people. I think that's where we are now."

GERBER CROUCHED near the arms locker, a can of C-rations in his hand. He stared at the concoction, which was a sickly yellow and tasted like bland paste. It had the same consistency, and all the salt in the world wouldn't help. He had once thought that the reason the Army supplied C-rations that needed generous amounts of salt added to make them edible, was that in the tropic environment it was impossible to get the men to eat enough salt. Now he decided it was just because no one cared enough to make the Cs edible. Who cared if a man twelve thousand miles away, without telephone support, didn't like his food?

Gerber set the OD can on the ground and looked at the rest of his meal. There was nothing in it that looked very good, but then he wasn't very hungry. He had been eating only because he figured he wouldn't have the opportunity for very much longer. After dark, he was going to be busy.

When a shadow fell across him, he looked up. "Hi, Robin. What can I do for you?"

She crouched next to him and then sat down, drew her knees up and wrapped her arms around her legs. "What's going to happen tonight?"

"What do you mean?"

"Come on, Mack, you know me. I've been here for a long time and I can see what's going on. You're preparing for an assault."

Gerber jammed his white plastic spoon into the remains of the scrambled eggs. "Kind of obvious, isn't it?"

"So what have you got?"

"Fetterman found signs of a large enemy force in the trees. Company-size or a little larger. We've had those new people coming in, none of whom look like your average farmer, and we've had an exodus of the locals."

"I talked to the people. They're tired of the war and the soldiers who fight it."

"And who blames them? But they've stayed here, even with all the trouble. We come in and find them in the ruins of a hamlet with little food and few possessions, but they're still here. Now, with their hootches being rebuilt and a new stock of food, they're getting out."

Morrow nodded but didn't speak.

"To me that means that someone has spread the word. This place is going to be attacked. The people getting out is one of the surest signs. Not to mention the signs that Fetterman found and the youngsters coming in."

"Tonight?"

Gerber shrugged. "Tonight. Tomorrow. It's going to happen soon. And even if they don't hit us tonight, we'll take some mortars and rockets."

"Then why don't you get out? Save everyone the horror of this?"

Gerber stared at her for a moment, not sure if she was serious or not. Finally he said, "Because that isn't one of the options I have. I can get you out now, if you want to go. I can get some of the women and children out, too, but I've got to stay."

"Then you're the one precipitating this fight."

"I suppose so, but how would pulling out help? You know me. If we can avoid this fight, tell me how."

She didn't look at him. "There are things I could say, but I think I'd regret them. I've talked to these people and I know what they think."

"Yes," said Gerber, "but that doesn't change the situation. Hell, Robin, you know we're here for more than just rebuilding the hamlet. We have to meet the challenge of the enemy forces. If we concede anything to them, then we've lost. They've picked the field."

"You can still get out."

"Except that another function of the military in war is to seek out the enemy, engage him and destroy him. Sometimes it's easier to let him seek you out and then destroy him, but it all comes down to the same thing. We're fighting a war."

He stopped talking and then added quickly, "That's what the media didn't understand about Tet. We let the enemy do the seeking, but then we destroyed him. All the figures aren't in yet, but the VC have been badly hurt. If we destroy enough of the enemy and his resources, he quits and then the people have what they want. The peace to live their lives."

"You really think it's that easy?"

"Robin, you know better than that. It's not easy, I never said it was. But think about it. We destroy the enemy, his capability to fight, his will to fight, and the war ends."

"So you're going to stay, regardless of what the people here want."

Gerber took a deep breath and tried to figure out what he was feeling. He knew Robin wasn't trying to make trouble. She was honestly interested in the situation and wanted honest answers. The problem was that Gerber didn't have any answers, though he was often called on to provide them.

"About the only thing I can say is that the people probably don't know what they want."

"To be left alone," she said. It wasn't a challenge. There was a sadness in her voice.

"Unfortunately," said Gerber, "that's the one thing they can't have, because the minute we pull out, the Vietcong will be in here. To gain that goal, we have to stay and fight."

"You believe this?"

"Robin, if I didn't believe it, I wouldn't be here. Someone, somewhere has to make a stand. If they don't, then those who feel they should dominate the world push to the front.

We've learned that lesson over and over, and yet we seem to forget it as quickly as we can."

Morrow stood and brushed the red dust from the seat of her pants. "I'm going to stay here."

"Yeah, I figured you would and I figured there'd be no way to get you out of here."

Now she smiled. "That tells me a lot, Mack. If you thought we didn't have a chance, you'd force me out of here."

"I think we'll take some mortars and there might be a ground probe, but they'll find we're too strong for them and retreat. Then the people will have the opportunity to live in peace. At least for a while."

"And you believe that?"

"Yes. Yes I do."

13

THE HAMLET OF DUC
BANG

The dull, flat bang echoed through the night. Shrapnel cut
through the air and debris rained down. Instinctively, Gerber threw himself to the ground, rolling toward the mud wall
of a hootch for the little additional protection it offered.

For a moment it was quiet, as if everything and everyone
had stopped. There was no sound from the animals, no
screams from the people and no firing. Gerber thought about
moving and hesitated. The whooshing sound came out of the
night, roared over his head and ended in another detonation
as the rocket destroyed itself.

"Incoming," someone shouted, already late with the
warning.

Gerber waited, listening, but there were no more rockets.
That was why he hated rockets. They were more powerful
and more deadly than mortars. There was no warning unless someone happened to see the flash as they fired. Suddenly, they were falling in the middle of your perimeter,
ripping apart the bunkers and the people.

There was shouting around him. He heard Helmsman's
voice cut through the night, but he couldn't see the young

officer. Finally Gerber was up and moving, hunched over like an old man fighting the wind. He headed toward the berm closest to the tree line and threw himself down there. He put his hands to his eyes, cupping his fingers around his brows to cut out the little light coming from the hamlet.

The trees were a black smudge, distinguishable against the lighter background of the sky. Moonlight reflected from the water in the paddies. Inside the trees, though, it was pitch-black, with neither the moon nor the stars helping. Gerber wished he had his binoculars, but wasn't sure they'd help.

"This the beginning?"

Gerber turned and saw Warren lying on the dirt beside him.

"I don't think so. Two rockets make a harassment raid and nothing more." Gerber looked at his watch. "Too early for Charlie. He's just letting us know he's out there."

Warren slipped down so that his head was no longer above the berm. He pulled his helmet off and wiped at the sweat on his forehead.

"You think they'll come at us tonight?"

"I think there's a real good chance there'll be some kind of probe," said Gerber. "But given the size of the force we've got here, I think we'll be able to handle it."

"Brave words, Captain. How will the slopes do?"

Now Gerber slipped away from the top of the berm. He stared at Warren and then said, "I think you'll find that the strikers we brought in are worth two or three of any Vietnamese soldiers you'd care to name, and I wouldn't let them hear you call them slopes."

"Didn't mean anything by it," said Warren.

And the funny thing, thought Gerber, was that he didn't. Everyone called the Vietnamese slopes or dinks or slants and no one thought about it. They didn't realize what it meant. That it was dehumanizing the Vietnamese. Maybe some soldiers needed to think that way so that they could shoot at the enemy. Maybe some of them thought that way because they hated the Vietnamese for the war. The strange thing was that if you asked any of them what the Vietnamese, the South Vietnamese, had done to them, they wouldn't have had an answer.

"I know you didn't," said Gerber, "but around our allies, let's watch our mouths. Before morning, we're liable to need their help and a number of them could die saving our asses."

"Yes, sir."

Gerber crawled higher again and studied the tree line. Still there was no movement in it. No lights and no sound.

"We need to get everyone on alert now," said Gerber. He slipped down and stood. "Make sure that everyone is at his place and that he's ready. We'll know if it's a big attack by the size of the opening barrage. They hit us hard and we'll know they're coming in force."

Almost as if to confirm what he said, Gerber could hear distant thunks as the rounds were fired from the tubes. Glancing at Warren, he said, "Mortars."

Instead of running for cover, Gerber threw himself against the berm, crawling higher so that he could watch the trees. He hoped Fetterman, Tyme and the rest of the men were doing the same.

The first round fell short, exploding in a rice paddy. There was an orange-yellow flash as the mortar threw up a cloud of smoke and a column of water. Gerber ducked as the second round exploded on the freshly turned soil that the bulldozer had raked up. Shrapnel whirled over his head and hit the soft earth of the berm. The odor of cordite filled the air, mingling with the smell of fresh dirt.

Gerber rolled down the berm and flattened himself on the ground as the next round landed in the hamlet. The whump of the explosion was louder than anything he'd ever heard. The heat of the detonation washed over him and he felt the shrapnel tug at his uniform, then pricklings of white-hot pain and splashes of wetness. He knew then that he'd been too close to that one.

In front of him, Warren lay on his back. His mouth was moving and his chest was heaving, but all Gerber could hear was the ringing in his ears. He glanced to the right and saw another round explode, but didn't hear it.

Then Gerber was on his feet, moving toward Warren. The big sergeant had taken shrapnel in the side. His jungle fatigues were ripped and there was blood all over them, but none of it was spurting.

"Christ, it burns," Warren said through clenched teeth.

Gerber bent close and examined the wounds. "You're not hit bad. Lots of blood, and it's good for a Purple Heart, but you'll live."

"Christ!"

Gerber dug at the first-aid kit that Warren wore on his pistol belt, shaking out one of the bandages. Using his knife, he cut away some of the cloth of Warren's uniform and pressed the bandage against the injured man's side.

"If you can get up, we can go find T.J. and let him take a look at you."

Warren nodded, then gritted his teeth. "Let's go."

Gerber helped Warren to his feet, but before they could move, the sergeant swayed. He grabbed onto Gerber's uniform and grunted. Gerber heard him and realized his hearing was slowly returning.

"You okay?" Gerber asked.

Warren didn't answer for a moment, then said. "Thought I was going to pass out."

They moved off. Gerber could hear the mortar rounds falling on the other side of the hamlet, but none was coming their way. As quickly as they could, they made their way toward the arms locker, which had been turned into a makeshift dispensary.

As they entered, Washington asked, "What've you got?"

"Warren took a little shrapnel."

"Sit him down over there," Washington said, nodding at a corner. "Figure I'm going to have a little business now." He moved toward the wounded man and then saw the blood on Gerber's uniform. "You hit, sir?"

"Caught a little shrapnel myself, but it's minor. I'll have you look me over later. I'm okay for now."

There was a sudden crash just outside the arms locker. They heard the shrapnel hit the concrete, bouncing off. Everyone dived to the floor, but no one was hurt. The rounds walked away from them.

"I'm going to find Sergeant Fetterman and Sergeant Tyme. If they've got anything spotted, I'll call in artillery."

"Yes, sir," said Washington. "Don't forget about those cuts. We don't want them to get infected."

"I'll watch myself," said Gerber.

FETTERMAN WAS CROUCHED at the edge of the berm, watching the tree line on the west side of the hamlet, when the first rocket slammed into the perimeter. As the second rocket ignited, he thought he saw the flash of the engine, but couldn't be sure. When the mortars started to fall, he saw the flash from the tubes.

"Yeah! Got it," he said. He slapped Tyme on the shoulder. "Over there. Again. See it?"

"Yeah, got it."

"Too bad we don't have some mortars of our own. Stir things up a bit."

"We could call in artillery. Captain's got them on alert," said Tyme.

The flashes came again. Fetterman flipped off the safety of his M-16 and opened fire. The whole magazine had been loaded with tracers. Twenty streaks of light flared into the trees where the mortar tubes were hidden.

As he fired, the perimeter near him opened up. M-16s and M-60s, all firing on full-auto, raked the trees. He saw some tracers disappearing into the darkness. He kept his eyes open and then the mortar fire ceased.

"That'll make them think twice," said Fetterman.

"We better get the men to cease fire. They're burning through the ammo pretty fast."

"We've got lots of it," said Fetterman.

The popping of the mortars came again, but this time from another location. He rolled to his right and watched the hamlet behind him, waiting for one or two of the rounds to land so he'd know where to go.

The explosion came from the center of the hamlet, near the arms locker.

"Hope T.J. had his head down," said Tyme.

The second round fell farther away. Fetterman breathed a sigh of relief, then said, "Let's go find Galvin and see if we can whistle up some of that arty support," he said. "Illumins and HE. Give Charlie something else to think about."

The firing from their side of the perimeter was beginning to taper off. Fetterman turned and yelled, "Cease fire! Cease fire."

"I don't understand this. The mortars were hidden in the trees. There's little chance that we'd hit anything."

"Son," said Fetterman, "you put enough rounds into the trees that way, and someone is bound to hit something. Besides, it tells Charlie that we've got a big force here. He sees us open up and waste ammo that way and he's going to think twice about hitting us."

They listened, but didn't hear any more mortars firing. They got to their feet and sprinted across the open ground behind the berm, running into the hamlet. Fetterman detoured long enough to make sure that everyone was okay in the dispensary and then headed over to where Bocker had set up the radios.

HELMSMAN WAS CROUCHED in the darkness behind one of the bunkers where his machine gunners were stationed. The bang of the rocket surprised and frightened him. He threw himself to the ground, his hands over his head, and listened as the second rocket exploded, throwing dirt and debris on him.

As soon as he could, he leaped to his feet and looked around wildly. He heard the mortars and knew what they were. Everyone who'd been in Vietnam for any length of time knew what they were, but unlike many of the men, Helmsman was terrified by mortars. He didn't know where they were going to land, or when, or how many there would be.

He stood flat-footed, trying to decide which way to run. Sweat beaded on his face and dripped down his sides, but it was not from the heat and humidity. It was fear. Fear of the mortars and the death raining down around him.

Firefights Helmsman could take, because he knew where the enemy was. He didn't mind grenades, because they were limited in their effectiveness by the strength of the man throwing them and by their small size. If the grenades were too big they couldn't be thrown far enough. But mortars, bombs falling out of the darkness, exploding into thousands of white-hot fragments that could rip a man apart—that was what frightened him.

The first round hit, off to the right, far from him. Helmsman was suddenly gripped with the urge to climb the berm and run down on the outside of the hamlet. The enemy wouldn't be aiming there and he wouldn't have to fear the mortars.

The second one hit, close this time, and Helmsman knew he was going to have to move. He whirled, saw the flash as another mortar detonated, then began to run. He ran along the perimeter, following it to the north. As soon as he was sure he was safe, he dived for cover, rolled once. Then he curled up into a ball, praying that the mortars would stop.

Helmsman lost his awareness of everything around him. He no longer heard the mortars and didn't hear the firing as Fetterman and Tyme tried to interdict the mortars. But he could feel the heat and the pain in his knees where he had scraped them as he fell to the ground. He could smell his own sweat and fear. He knew he wasn't acting like an Army officer, but it was the damned mortars. Even the human wave attack that he feared would be better than the mortars. He could do something about the human wave attack, but he was powerless against the mortars.

ROBIN LOOMED OUT of the darkness in one corner of the arms locker. She saw Gerber crouching near Warren and hurried to him. She touched his shoulder and felt the wetness there.

"You okay?" she asked, her voice filled with fear.

"I'm fine," he responded. "Got clipped by some shrapnel, but it's nothing."

There was firing from the perimeter. Morrow looked toward it, as if she could see something through the solid, concrete wall of the arms locker.

"That's our people," said Gerber.

"How can you tell?"

"Sound of the weapons. M-16s and M-60s make a distinctive sound. We're not taking incoming rifle fire."

Morrow crouched and said, "Then what are they shooting at?"

"Probably at the tree lines, hoping to take out some of the mortar men."

"There's something else you should know," she said suddenly, as if she hadn't heard the last thing that Gerber had said.

"What's that?"

"The villagers are almost all gone. There can't be more than a dozen left, not counting those people who came in this afternoon."

"That's it, then," Gerber said. "It's on for tonight. We can expect them to try and force us out of here tonight."

"What are you going to do?"

Gerber shrugged and realized that she wouldn't be able to see the gesture in the dark. "I'm going to find Bocker and see if we can call in artillery on the tree lines. If we can drop a few rounds on the staging points before they can get going, we might be able to break up the attack."

"What are our chances?"

"Shit, Robin, we're really in good shape. There's what, fifty, sixty Americans here if you count the Seabees, and they're supposed to be fighters as well as engineers. And we've a hundred strikers. We've a new barricade for Charlie to climb and he has to assault over two hundred yards of open ground. There shouldn't be a problem."

The firing on the line tapered off and then ended completely. The mortars stopped exploding, and it was quiet for a moment. Silence swept in and Morrow suddenly felt strange. There was an eerie feeling all around, like the sudden quiet before a storm broke. The air was hot and heavy with no breeze. There were no animals around, no sounds of insects. It was an utter and total silence except for the quiet moan of the wounded who shared the arms locker with her and Gerber.

And then the world seemed to explode. A gigantic bang ripped through the air. The concussion shook the walls of the arms locker. Dust clouds rose into the air and people were coughing.

"What the hell?" said Morrow.

"Satchel charge. I think our visitors have just made their first move."

"What are you going to do?" asked Morrow.

"Look for Fetterman. Then get the artillery started so Charlie can't get at us." Gerber snagged his rifle and started for the door.

He crouched there for a moment, surveying the outside, barely visible in the light of a sliver-thin moon and thousands of stars. Morrow joined him and touched his shoulder again.

"Be careful, Mack."

"Always," he said as he launched himself from the door, running for the bunker line.

THE BANQUET HALL LOOKED like something out of the Middle Ages. A single long table occupied the center of the room with twenty high-backed chairs on either side. At each end of the table was a massive chair, larger than the ones ranged on the sides. In front of each place at the table was a full dinner setting. Flags hung from poles mounted on the walls at a forty-five-degree angle. A huge crystal chandelier was suspended from the ceiling forty feet above the table. Armed guards were stationed at all doors, half of them Vietnamese rangers in their finest uniforms, the other half American Marines dressed in their blues.

Padgett sat halfway down the table flanked by two women he didn't know. One of them was Vietnamese, though she had some European blood, and the other was a woman from the embassy, obviously invited so that the ratio of men to women would be more even.

He'd worked his way through the first few courses, choosing the correct forks and spoons and knives without having to watch the others around him. He'd used his fingers where proper, had proposed one toast, as he had been ordered to do, and was now engaged in conversation with the Eurasian woman. He was sweating, even though a massive air conditioner somewhere was keeping the hall cool by tropical standards.

Padgett dabbed at his forehead with his napkin, wiping away the sweat. He could feel sweat dripping down his sides and under his arms. This was the kind of occasion that he feared the most—a formal state dinner to welcome the congressmen. Padgett was painfully aware that the Vietnamese politicians and military brass were watching every move. A slipup, no matter how small, could end his career. After a day of playing that game, Padgett was ready for a leisurely meal. He was not ready for a state dinner.

"So, General, what is it that you do?" the Vietnamese woman asked.

Padgett grinned. "It's nothing too important or interesting, I'm afraid. I coordinate the civic action projects that are being administered by the Army, making sure that each project is treated fairly and that none are overlooked."

"It sounds like a job that is beneficial, not destructive as so many of the military occupations are."

"I think," said Padgett, "you'll find that many military occupations are beneficial, and even those that are destructive can be selective about that destruction. In the long run, very little of the military is destructive."

"Oh?"

"Certainly." Padgett grinned again, self-consciously this time. "Even World War II, one of the most destructive wars ever fought, proved to be beneficial in the end. A worldwide threat was eliminated, and both Japan and Germany have prospered since the war."

"You're not suggesting that we fight a war so that we can rebuild our country from the ground up?"

"No, of course not. I'm merely suggesting that the destructive power of the military is more than countered by the good things it accomplishes."

"I believe that is a very narrow view," she said.

Padgett wanted to agree with her, but felt pressed to defend the military. He knew of all the things wrong with it, but the problems weren't as clear-cut as the civilians wanted them to be. It wasn't the military that started wars, but whoever was responsible, it was the soldiers who paid a high price. He realized that civilian casualties were running above those suffered by the armies involved, but it still wasn't the armed forces that had wanted the war. Now they were involved in it, their attitude was that it was the only war they had.

Still, having spent his life building his career in the military, he didn't like people who didn't bother to understand the situation, condemning him because of his uniform. For those reasons he felt himself pressed into defending points of view that he didn't really believe.

Padgett shrugged in response to the woman's comment, because he didn't know what to say. He concentrated on his food. He didn't know who his partner was, or how much power she might have. The last thing he wanted to do was irritate a woman whose husband or boyfriend might have a high position in the local government and who then could make trouble for him. Military careers had been destroyed over less.

He was saved from having to continue the conversation, when a man dressed in jungle fatigues entered the hall, stopped and talked to one of the American guards. After scanning the table, he worked his way to Padgett, bent close and said, "I have a message for you, General." He handed Padgett a folded piece of paper.

"How long ago did this come in?"

"Ten minutes, sir."

Padgett plucked his napkin from his lap, patted his lips and stood up. He bowed to the woman on his right and then to his left. "If you'll excuse me, something has come up."

"I hope it is nothing too serious," said the Vietnamese woman. "I had looked forward to completing our discussion before you had to leave."

"So did I, but it's a truly pressing matter, something they feel that only I can remedy. I hope you will forgive me for deserting you."

"Of course, General. Maybe you'll have the opportunity to return in time for dessert."

"A distinct possibility."

"Good evening, General."

"Good evening."

He left the banquet hall with the messenger right behind him. As soon as they were in the corridor, he turned and said, "How do we know we've lost radio contact with Duc Bang?"

"Transmission broke off in the middle of a message and we haven't been able to raise them again."

"Maybe they had a radio failure."

"But they had more than one radio, especially after the Seabees arrived. We think something has gone wrong there and they can't make radio contact."

"Shit!" said Padgett. "That's all we need with a congressional delegation here."

14

THE HAMLET OF DUC BANG

"We've got a major problem," said Fetterman. He was crouched next to the remains of a hootch, his M-16 clutched in one hand.

"What's that?" Gerber asked. He could barely make out Fetterman's face in the darkness. There was a sheen to it, suggesting that the master sergeant was sweating, something that he rarely did.

"Bocker's down. I've got Tyme and Santini taking him to the dispensary. I don't know how bad he's hurt."

"What in the hell happened?"

"We found him lying in the dirt, the remains of the radios around him. Someone hit him on the back of the head, then destroyed the radios."

Gerber touched his lips with his hand. He stared at Fetterman. "You get any kind of message out?"

"I'd told Bocker to alert the people in Saigon that we thought something was going to happen tonight, but no one made any arrangements in case we lost radio contact. Hell, sir, we had so many, it didn't seem to matter."

"Anyone looking at the radios?"

"One of the Seabees said he knew something about electronics and might be able to cobble something together, but I'm not holding my breath."

"That means we're on our own now. Shit, that was not what I had in mind."

"Yes, sir."

"Let's get the Vietnamese rounded up and under guard. Obviously we can't trust them."

"I'll get Tyme and Santini and see what we can do."

Gerber nodded and took a single step. In the distance came a constant string of pops as if someone had dumped a carton of light bulbs on the ground—it was the sound of mortar rounds firing. Gerber stood there for a moment, staring into the distance, but the berm screened the trees from him so that he couldn't see the mortar tubes.

"We're going to have to wait for a moment."

"Yes, sir."

Together they took off, running for the perimeter. They stopped outside one of the machine gun bunkers. It had a layer of sandbags on top of it, then a layer of logs and finally another layer of sandbags. The idea was to detonate the mortars high. They didn't have the power of rockets and couldn't punch through to the men inside.

Gerber stepped down into the bunker. There was a dim orange light in the corner, where a man was smoking, shielding the cigarette so that it wouldn't be visible through the firing port.

"Incoming!" Gerber yelled as the first rounds began to drop.

The first detonations were outside the perimeter, but the VC gunners quickly found the range. The rounds began to drop like rain, landing in the hamlet, raking the interior with hot shrapnel. It slammed into the side of the bunker.

Gerber sat down on an ammo can to watch the trees across the open rice paddies. Fetterman crouched opposite him in order to monitor the other end.

Over the noise of the falling mortars Fetterman said, "We could put some rounds into the trees."

The gunner cranked the bolt, ejecting a live round and then waited for an order.

"Go ahead," said Gerber.

The man swung the barrel around and aimed over the open fields. He pressed the butterfly trigger and the weapon fired a short burst. The hot brass ejected, rattling against the planks on the inside of the bunker. The muzzle-flash stabbed out into the night. Gerber turned his head so he wouldn't ruin his night vision.

The mortars kept coming. The detonations ran together into a single, long explosion. Gerber moved back from the firing port and knelt in the entrance of the bunker. He stayed back, letting the sandbags protect him, and listened as the enemy hammered the hamlet. He wished he could communicate with others on the line and hoped his men had taken charge. There was nothing he could do until the mortars stopped. As long as they were falling, he could at least be sure the enemy wasn't going to attack.

MORROW HUDDLED in a corner of the arms locker and listened to the world blow up around her. She pulled the remains of an ammo crate toward her and rolled close to the wall. There was a partial roof above her, but the first round to hit would demolish it. One more day would have allowed the men to finish getting the bunkers ready. As it was, there weren't enough usable bunkers.

"You okay, Miss Morrow?" came Washington's voice.

"Yes, I'm fine." She was surprised how strong her voice sounded. She could feel the cold sweat of fear and her stomach was flipping in her belly. She was scared, but tried not to show it. She kept thinking that she didn't have to be there. All she'd had to do was call her boss and tell him she had a story and she would have been on the way home. But, no, she had to try and show up all the male reporters on the staff.

The mortars continued to fall, but they weren't landing near the arms locker. It sounded as if the enemy had targeted the bunker line and were having some success keeping rounds landing in that area.

There was a groan from the entrance and a man fell into the locker.

Morrow sat up, where she could see what was happening. The man was on his hands and knees, his head down. He shook it, like a dog that had just been soaked. "Medic!"

Washington hurried to the man and tried to lift him to his feet to take him deeper into the locker. Morrow, too, moved to help Washington.

"I'm hit," said the man.

Morrow recognized him as Helmsman. The lieutenant's back was covered with blood. His fatigue shirt was shredded. She took his arm as Washington guided him toward a cot, letting him lie on his stomach.

With his combat knife Washington ripped away the remains of the shirt. Then, holding his fingers over the lens of a flashlight so that he didn't let much light escape, he examined the wounded man.

Washington looked at Morrow. "Get me some of the sterile gauze."

Morrow turned and began rummaging through the big medical kit Washington had brought to Duc Bang. She pulled out one of the huge bandages and ripped open its sterile wrapper. As she shook it out, she watched Washington work.

"You're going to be okay," he told Helmsman. "Just some shrapnel." He grabbed a piece that was protruding from Helmsman's back. As he wrenched it free, Helmsman grunted with pain.

"We'll get you wrapped up and then let you rest here. The doctors at the evac hospital will have to dig out the rest of the shrapnel. I can't do it."

"Is that going to be a problem?" asked Morrow.

"Nah," he told her, then turned back to Helmsman. "You could hit the line again, if you feel up to it."

Sounding as if he had run a mile, Helmsman said, "I need to rest for a moment."

Outside, the mortars started coming closer again. The pounding that the perimeter had taken was now being directed at the interior of the hamlet. Morrow crouched next to the wall of the arms locker, her face against the rough cool concrete.

GERBER HEARD when the mortars shifted to a new target area, and leaped through the bunker door. He knelt there for a moment, looking at the fires that now burned in the hamlet. Some of them marked the remains of bunkers that had taken four or five direct hits. Others were from the hootches that had been partially repaired during the day, flames leaping twenty feet into the air, as the dry thatch and plywood burned brightly. In the flickering light, Gerber saw that the ground was covered with debris. Broken bits of wood, tin, sandbags and rocks were everywhere. There were small craters created by the exploding mortars.

Gerber ran along the line. He found all the men in one bunker had been killed. The air was heavy with the odor of fresh copper, smelling like the inside of a slaughterhouse.

From another bunker came a quiet moaning. Gerber made his way to it, keeping his head down. He crouched there for an instant and then began digging through the rubble. He found one of the Navy men, but as he tried to lift him out, the wounded man shrieked with sudden pain.

Gerber let go and jumped into the bunker. He found the man's leg was caught under a beam, and as he lifted the beam clear, the man groaned again. Blood spurted from the gaping wound in his leg. Without hesitation, Gerber stripped the man's web belt from his pants and looped it over the leg, drawing it tight. The flow of blood slowed.

"Medic," Gerber yelled. "Medic!"

A dark shape appeared. "What's happening?"

"Get this man over to the dispensary. He's got a massive wound in the leg."

Together they lifted him, then the medic carried him off, into the darkness.

The mortars shifted again, coming back to the bunker line. Gerber knelt in the bunker, watching the explosions as they came toward him and then diving for cover as they passed over him to fall harmlessly in the open fields outside the camp.

Suddenly it was silent. The mortars had stopped. Then the shouting began. Men screaming for help, yelling for the medic or calling to God. There were shouts of anger and fear and panic. The men at the bunker line began to fire, first only a few, then nearly everyone as they tried to get even.

In the distance Gerber heard shouts and bugles and whistles. The attack was beginning. He pushed his way to the front of his ruined bunker and stared into the darkness. He needed artillery support and illumination and he had none. Then he remembered those VC who'd entered the hamlet pretending to be farmers. He had to do something about them, or the Americans would find themselves in real trouble.

Before he could turn and look back into the hamlet, the tree line erupted and the enemy poured into the paddies, firing from their hips. Their muzzle-flashes sparkled like fireflies on a hot summer evening. Green tracers lanced through the air, slamming into the berm and bouncing high, tumbling. Red tracers answered, weaving a multicolored net over the open paddies.

The M-79s thumped, and the grenades fell among the enemy in spark-filled fountains of flame. The enemy went down, but there were others to take their places.

The firing increased in tempo until it was a loud, continuous roar punctuated by explosions from grenades. But, Gerber held his fire. He moved from his position at the front of the bunker and turned, watching the hamlet behind him.

Inside the hamlet, he caught movement, two or three people dodging from hootch to hootch. They stopped short, using the last of the protection of the hamlet. Without warning, they opened fire, raking the inside of the bunker line with AK-47s.

Gerber didn't hesitate. He aimed and fired, emptying a magazine into them. They all went down in the burst.

FETTERMAN SAW THE ASSAULT being mounted at the edge of the trees and directed his aim there, firing on semi-auto as fast as he could pull the trigger. He pumped rounds into the trees, aiming low. Next to him, the M-60 began to fire, the chattering overwhelming the bugles in the trees.

There was a flickering in the distance, and the tree line seemed to shift as the men ran from it. Firing as they ran, they filled the night with muzzle-flashes and green tracers. Fetterman didn't have to order the men to shoot back. The bunker line opened fire and the war became a Technicolor nightmare of eerie shapes and bright lights.

The men of the attacking force died quickly, falling into the shallow water of the rice paddies. Others took their places, running along the dikes and then leaping into the paddies to protect themselves. The firing from the Vietcong surged and ebbed like the tide. Volume rose and fell, the shooting becoming an overwhelming din and then dropping off until it sounded like two men dueling.

There was a sudden burst behind Fetterman. He heard the bullets ripping into the sandbags there. As he whirled, a sustained burst came from another bunker and the firing stopped.

Fetterman turned his attention to the enemy. They had made it halfway across the open paddies, but the race for the perimeter had stopped. Those still living fell to the ground, using the dikes as breastworks. They propped their weapons there and held down the triggers, burning through their ammo. Fetterman knew an attacking force couldn't carry that much spare ammo, and when they ran out, they'd be sitting ducks for the defenders.

The machine gunner had stopped firing short bursts, and was just holding the trigger down as the assistant fed the belts through the weapon. When they finally ran out of belts, the barrel was glowing a dull red. The weapon was now useless.

But that didn't matter because the attack had been halted. The enemy was pinned down between the safety of the trees and the perimeter of the hamlet. If the Americans could have called in artillery, it would have been a slaughter.

The firing had slowed as if both sides were running out of steam. Fetterman leaped from the back of the bunker and ran along the rear of the bunker line, shouting at the men to use their grenade launchers, urging them to fire into the rice paddies. He got the grenadiers into action, and the M-79s pumped grenades into the fields, the explosions dotting the paddies.

Fetterman came to Gerber, crouched in the rear of the bunker, still watching the hamlet.

"Got three of them," Gerber said.

Fetterman looked at the sprawled bodies. "Yes, sir, I see that."

"You seem to have things under control here," said Gerber. "I think I'll be more useful elsewhere."

"Yes, sir."

Gerber vaulted from the bunker and disappeared into the interior of the hamlet. Fetterman continued down the line, keeping low, as the enemy and the strikers exchanged shots while trying not to get killed.

He reached the end of the line and found that everyone in the corner bunker had been wounded. Two of them had taken shrapnel and one had been shot. None was hurt badly and they still manned their weapons.

He started back along the line. From the interior of the hamlet came a wild burst of firing and he hoped that Gerber hadn't walked into something. He wanted to go check, but couldn't leave the bunkers. He knew the enemy would soon realize they had to move. To stay where they were was inviting disaster.

SANTINI WATCHED as the Navy man pulled all the parts from the various radios together and examined them in the beam of his flashlight. He'd taken out the red lens so that he could study the color-coded wires.

The mortar barrage had slowed and moved away from them, then stopped all together. Santini wanted to point to parts, to take over the task, but didn't. He stood behind the man, watching the activity as firing began on the perimeter.

"They're coming," Santini said.

"I'm working as fast as I can."

"You think you'll be able to get something working in the next few minutes?"

The man shot a glance over his shoulder and snapped, "I won't get anything done if you keep asking me a bunch of dumb questions."

Santini was going to respond, but realized it would do no good. He wished Bocker was conscious because he had more faith in the Special Forces sergeant. He'd seen Bocker take nothing more than some wire, a battery and what seemed to be dirt, twigs and seashells and make a working radio. The Navy guy just seemed to be picking at the broken radios, doing nothing but looking at them as he shook his head.

Santini heard a sound behind him and whirled, dropping to one knee. In the darkness, he saw the tiny shape of one of the Vietnamese. She came forward slowly, her hands empty. As she neared, she began to unbutton her shirt, her teeth flashing in the night.

"You like, GI?" she asked.

Santini didn't understand for a moment. Why would she suddenly turn affectionate in the middle of an attack? And then he understood completely.

She grabbed at the waistband of her shorts. Santini didn't wait. He whipped the barrel of his M-16 around and pulled the trigger three times. The rounds slammed into her midriff, driving her back. She grunted in pain and surprise as she tossed into the air the pistol she had concealed in her shorts. She dropped to her back, the blood spreading across her belly.

Santini moved toward her and as he did, she groaned. She tried to roll to her side and began clawing her way toward the pistol she'd dropped. Santini stepped closer and brought his foot down on her hand. As he did, she turned her head and looked up at him. For a moment it looked as if she was going to speak. Instead she coughed. Blood poured from her mouth as she died.

Santini moved to the door of the hootch and looked out. There was no one else around. The Vietnamese were beginning to spread out through the hamlet, trying to do what they could to disrupt the defense. He hoped the rest of them had the same kind of luck.

THE BUGLES STARTED AGAIN, the sound drifting across open rice paddies and the men who were hiding there. Fetterman dropped to the ground, then climbed up the berm and peeked over the top. Firing from the rice paddies increased, as if the men trapped there were protecting the men coming from the trees.

There was hesitation in the bunkers, and then firing began along the line. The enemy appeared at the tree line, a shadowy army protected by the darkness and the first wave now pinned down. Fetterman pushed the barrel of his rifle over the top of the berm, but didn't fire. Instead, he watched as the second wave swept out of the gloom, leaped over the first and kept on coming.

More firing began and the sound swelled until it was a roar. Vietcong ran forward, stumbled and fell. They returned fire, their green tracers looping toward the hamlet.

Fetterman slipped from his position and ran along the berm to the corner. He dropped into the bunker there. One dead man was lying on the floor covered with blood. The smell of fresh copper was all around. Fetterman stepped over the body so that he could see out of the firing port.

The machine gun with the burned barrel stood silent. The men were using their M-16s, firing on full-auto, cranking the rounds through as fast as they could. The spent brass and emptied magazines covered the floor and were piling up.

"Cease fire!" ordered Fetterman. "Cease fire! Cease fire!" He kept saying it until the men in the bunker stopped shooting and stood there looking at him.

"Semi-auto. Everyone fire on semi-auto so we don't ruin the rifles."

Fetterman knelt and began to fire through the port. He shot in slow motion, trying to set an example for the men with him. The enemy was still struggling through the rice paddies, but hadn't gotten close to the hamlet.

One man ran along the dike, a pistol in one hand and a whistle in the other. Fetterman aimed and fired. The man kept coming and Fetterman fired a second time. The enemy soldier stopped, clutched a hand to his chest and fell to his knees. He remained there for a moment, then toppled into the water with a small splash.

The enemy fire seemed to increase then. The air was filled with the tracers and the muzzle-flashes blended into a long, flickering light that marked the progress of the enemy soldiers.

Fetterman flipped his selector to full-auto because the VC had crossed the paddies and were now running over the clear area created by the bulldozer. He fired in short three- and four-round bursts, watching the enemy soldiers fall and die. The men with him followed suit. The noise and heat in the bunker increased. The smell of burned gunpowder overpowered the smell of blood from the dead man. Fetterman felt the sweat bead and drip as he watched the enemy. The air was becoming too close, and he was afraid that the firing would consume the last of the oxygen.

GERBER WORKED HIS WAY into the center of the hamlet, keeping low and using the remains of the hootches for cover. He let his eyes adjust to the dark, trying to pick out human shapes. He came to one man sprawled on the ground. There was the unmistakable odor of death around him. Gerber picked up the man's dropped M-16 so the enemy wouldn't get it. He continued on, searching.

He turned to the north, moving from one hootch to the next. There were a few shapes moving, but he identified them. Tyme was on the run, heading across the compound toward the bunker where Fetterman fought. He'd left Sully Smith in charge of the strikers on the side of the perimeter opposite the action.

Gerber stopped him and asked, "What's it look like?"

"Dead, sir. Strikers antsy to get into the action, but we've held them tight. Just in case."

"Watch out for the Vietnamese who came in late. They're definitely VC."

"How do you know?"

"Three of them opened fire on the bunker line. I killed them, but keep your eyes open."

"Yes, sir."

As Tyme raced for the bunker line, Gerber continued his hunt. He heard the bugles and the whistles and the firing increase on the perimeter, and knew that another push was being made, but he also knew that Fetterman could handle it. He had to find the enemy soldiers.

Then, along the bunker line, he saw four shapes moving. They halted and conferred. One of them broke from the group and ran forward, carrying something. He tossed it at the corner bunker and threw himself to the ground. In that moment, Gerber knew they were the enemy.

He flipped his weapon to full-auto and opened fire. Three figures went down in sprawling, rolling heaps. The other failed to move. The bunker in front of Gerber exploded then, a loud sound that drove him back. The flash was blinding and he lost sight of the Vietnamese who had been hiding.

Gerber heard an AK open fire. He dived to his right, squeezing his eyes shut. When he opened them, he stared into the night, but the enemy soldier was gone. Gerber crawled to the remains of a wall. He peeked over the top, but didn't see the man. He rolled to the left and tried again. There was a flicker of movement and another burst from the AK.

Gerber returned fire and heard a shriek of pain. It was an old trick: make the enemy think you're wounded so he stupidly stands up. Gerber didn't fall for it. Instead, he crawled farther to the left until he reached the end of the wall.

Around the corner, he spotted the man. Nothing more than a dark shape against a darker background, but he could see the weapon, the shape distinctive. He grinned to himself and opened fire, squeezing off a five-round burst.

The rounds struck the man in the side. He spasmed in surprise, flipping his weapon away from him. He rolled over and then was still. With that, Gerber was on his feet. He sprinted to the downed man and checked for a pulse. He found none.

As he moved back into the hamlet, the firing on the opposite perimeter grew in intensity. At that moment he knew he had to get back there, because it sounded as if the world was ending. If they didn't catch a few breaks, it could be the end. Gerber turned and ran for the perimeter.

15

HOTEL THREE, SAIGON

Padgett stood in the terminal, smoking his pipe, while he waited for the chopper that had been ordered to pick him up. He had changed to jungle fatigues, flak jacket and helmet. A .45 was slung on his hip with a canteen and a first-aid kit. Collins, who stood next to him, looked like a man planning on a war. He carried an M-16 with four bandoliers of ammo, had a .45 along with spare magazines, a canteen, flak jacket and helmet.

The chopper touched down on one of the helipads and the crew chief leaped clear. He ran to the terminal still wearing his chicken plate and his flight helmet trailing the black cord that would plug him into the intercom system. He wore an Old West-style holster with a .38 in it.

"General Padgett?" he shouted as he approached.

"I'm Padgett."

"Follow me, General." The man spun and ran toward the chopper. He stopped by the skids and waited until both Padgett and Collins had climbed on board. As he plugged his helmet into the intercom, he handed a helmet to Padgett. The general plugged into a separate system, set up so that the men in the back could speak directly to the pilots or on any of the radios. It was the C and C setup used by most aviation companies.

Once Padgett was on line, he said, "Do you know where we need to go?"

The aircraft commander turned in his seat and looked into the cargo compartment. "Yes, sir. We got a briefing in Operations before takeoff."

"Then let's get going."

The pilot swiveled and took the controls. He reached down and turned a knob on the radio control head. A moment later they took off, climbing into the darkness. To the east, out the left door of the chopper, were the lights of Saigon. From the air at night, it hardly looked like a city of war. The lights blazed, making it a prime target. Enemy gunners had only to aim at the glow in the distance when they fired their rockets, though since Tet, they hadn't fired many into the city.

In stark contrast, out the right door, it was black. Only a few lights dotted the land. Far to the south, the ground seemed brighter, where the moon and stars reflected from the water of the swamps. Highway 1 stretched like a long black ribbon to the west.

They turned to follow it, dodging south of the American base at Cu Chi, another bright spot in the sea of blackness. Once around it, they turned to the northwest, flying toward Dau Tieng at fifteen hundred feet. The nav lights were on steady dim and the rotating beacon flashed, but they would be nearly invisible from the ground.

The helicopter crossed Dau Tieng at three thousand feet, avoiding the traffic pattern for the airfield there, continuing its journey to the northwest. Finally the pilot came on the intercom and said, "General, my instructions from this point are sketchy. Are we to land at Duc Bang?"

"No. Not yet. I want to fly over and scope out the situation. We've lost radio contact and don't know why."

"We're about five out now," said the AC. He pointed through the windshield. "Duc Bang should be out in that direction."

Padgett shifted around so that he could see better. As he watched, he saw the tracers flashing. Red going out and green going in. Streaks of light that marked the position of the hamlet as precisely as an arrow on the ground. There was a flickering brightness from the dozens of small fires burning inside the perimeter.

"Do we have to land?"

"No," said Padgett. "I have my answer."

GERBER HAD FOUND Fetterman standing behind the corner bunker, firing his weapon as fast as he could pull the trigger. The machine guns around them hammered out a steady stream of fire. The enemy was rushing forward, screaming and shouting and shooting. They were scrambling to climb the berm around the perimeter.

One VC reached the top, but before he could do anything, he was shot again and again, his riddled body falling outside the hamlet. There were explosions among the bunkers, and the firing seemed to increase in volume. The sounds ran together and became a roar. Shouts and shots and bugles and whistles filled the air. Explosions from the underpowered Chicom grenades and louder, flatter detonations from the M-79s added to the noise. Lights sparkled and flickered and the night took on a strange brightness that had a life of its own.

Gerber dropped to one knee and fired his weapon in four- and five-round bursts, burning through his magazines. Consciously, he aimed low, knowing that the tendency at night was to fire high. He emptied one magazine, jerked it from his weapon and tossed it aside. He slammed another home and began to shoot again.

The enemy had reached the center of the area cleared by the bulldozer. A few of the braver men crossed most of it, dying at the foot of the redoubt. Only one man had climbed it and that had cost him his life.

Then, with no order given, the enemy ranks broke. They turned and fled, running back the way they had come. Dozens of their friends lay in the open, some of them floating in the rice paddies, others on the dikes and the remainder on the cleared ground at the foot of the berm. They had not succeeded in penetrating the perimeter, though they had destroyed part of it with their grenades and satchel charges and had killed or wounded a portion of the defenders.

Gerber took a few potshots at the fleeing men and then lowered his weapon. Firing on the line decreased slowly until it was only sporadic, with the exception of a single machine gun. The rounds slammed into the trees, but there was no return file. Finally it, too, fell silent, and the only sounds were the groaning of the wounded and the quiet chatter of men as they talked to one another.

Gerber slipped down the berm and sat there for a moment, breathing deeply. Without thinking, he pulled the partially used magazine from his weapon, looked into it and then replaced it with a full one. He felt the heat and humidity of the night, and became aware of the sweat soaking his uniform. There was grit on his face and hands—some of it from the extended firing of his weapon and some of it dirt from the compound.

Fetterman joined him. "They'll be back."

"Christ, Tony, you sound like a character in a bad Western talking about the Indians."

"Yes, sir. We're going to be in trouble on the next one, if they've got another company in there. We've taken some serious damage."

Gerber glanced to the right and saw that a number of bunkers were again smoking ruins. There were bodies lying behind a few of them. Men worked over the wounded while others scrambled to make repairs before the enemy came again.

Gerber got to his feet. "I'll see if we can't get one of the radios working for support. That'll make the difference."

"Check on Galvin. He'll get one of them working, somehow," said Fetterman.

Gerber had taken one step, when firing erupted inside the perimeter. Men lying behind the partial protection of a hootch wall opened up on the soldiers trying to help their wounded friends. A few of them fell, hit in the sudden burst. Others dived for cover.

Gerber rolled to one side, but didn't fire. He shot a glance at Fetterman and the two of them were up and moving. They ran to the south, hurdled a short wall and dropped to the ground. Gerber crawled to one edge of the wall while Fetterman took the other. They didn't have to speak because each knew what had to be done and how to do it. They worked in perfect unity, each taking one half of the mission.

The firing tapered and stopped, but that made no difference to them. They saw where the enemy was hidden. Gerber moved first, crawling across the open ground, hidden by the lay of the land, the standing walls of the bombed-out hootch and the darkness. As soon as he was under cover again, Fetterman began to work his way forward.

The two of them moved closer to the enemy soldiers until the VC could be seen easily. As the two Americans rose to shoot, the enemy spotted them and rushed forward. Both men opened fire, on semi-auto, picking the targets.

Gerber was hit by a figure leaping at him. The soldier clawed at the captain's face. Gerber rolled with the enemy, grappled and then swung his rifle around, firing once, the muzzle buried in the VC's stomach. The shriek of surprise and pain told Gerber he had shot a woman. She rolled away, doubled into a ball with her hands clutching at the wound. She continued to scream in agony.

Gerber spun around to face a second adversary, but Fetterman had slipped under the outstretched arms. As the VC fell past him, Fetterman struck him in the back of the head with the butt of the M-16, forcing the man to the ground. As he rolled, Fetterman shot and killed him.

Now all the enemy soldiers inside the hamlet were down. Gerber knelt beside the woman, whose screams had turned into grunts of pain and panic. She reached toward him with one blood-covered hand and died.

Fetterman checked the others and found that they were all dead. "Five," he said. "That takes care of at least five of them."

Gerber nodded, the gesture hard to see in the dark. "There's only one left now, unless someone else killed him. I already got several of them."

Together they ran back to the bunker line. They split up then, checking each bunker and the men inside. A dozen had been carried to the dispensary. Twelve more were dead, laid out behind the bunkers, waiting for Graves Registration to pick them up.

The damage had been heavy, but the line was still defensible, if the Vietcong didn't have too many men held in reserve and didn't want to win so badly they would use unlimited troops and arms. They could hold off another attack, but then everything would be up for grabs.

Gerber found Fetterman. "If we move half the men from other points on the perimeter, we can hold here."

"And if they hit two sides at once?"

"If they have the force to do that, we're fucked, no matter what we do. We shift the men now, we'll be in a better position to hold. We'll just have to remain flexible."

"Yes, sir. I'll find Tyme and Smith and coordinate that."

"No, Tony, you stay here. I'll do it. I want to check on the radios, too."

"Yes, sir."

As Fetterman turned to reorganize the bunker line, Gerber started across the hamlet. He'd reached the first line of hootches when the bugles blew again. A single, searing note that cut through the night like a knife. He spun and ran back to the bunker line, wanting to see the size of the enemy force.

Then, as the Vietcong began to attack out of the trees, the world around them exploded into fire and shrapnel, and the attack died before it had a chance to begin.

THE SCENE BELOW PADGETT was obvious. Somehow, all the radios of the men on the ground had been destroyed. They couldn't call for help. The general keyed the mike. "What's the nearest artillery advisory?"

Before the pilot could answer, Collins was on the intercom, asking, "What are you planning to do, sir?"

"I'm calling artillery in on the enemy, Captain. What did you think I was going to do?"

"But, sir, we don't know where our men are."

"Don't be stupid, Collins. Our men are in the hamlet and the bad guys are in the trees. Look down there. You can see it marked as clearly as if we used a map."

"They might have patrols out."

"And if they do, the poor men on the patrols are probably already dead. What the fuck do you use patrols for? To find the enemy. I think Gerber and his boys have already located the enemy."

"How do you know—"

"Collins, are you that dumb? I don't need radio contact to tell me the situation on the ground. The hamlet is burning. You have red tracers going out and green going in. You understand?"

The pilot broke in. "I've got us dialed in for the arty."

"Thank you." Padgett glared at Collins, but the captain refused to speak again. Padgett made contact with the arty advisory and told them he had a fire mission for them. It would require HE and there were no friendlies within two or three hundred yards of the kill zone.

There was a response from the Spec Four at the other end and then he said, "Shot, over."

Padgett replied, "Shot, out." He looked at Collins. "I haven't called artillery in on anybody since the Korean War." There was a lightness in his voice. It felt good to be back in the action rather than reading about other men who were doing the brave deeds.

There was a bright, mushrooming blast on the ground. White phosphorus lit up the sky just short of the trees. Padgett made his adjustment and then yelled, "Fire for effect."

A moment later, the tree line exploded. Balls of orange burst among the trees. The enemy fired into the night sky, but they were shooting blind, not even close.

"On target," Padgett yelled in his excitement. "Pour it to them."

The artillery kept falling in the trees. Padgett watched as the chopper circled to the south of the tree line and the hamlet, well outside the gun target lines. He saw only the flashes of fire as the rounds detonated, ripping up the landscape and killing the enemy soldiers. Without contact on the ground, he didn't know how long to keep it up. When the arty advisory asked him for a report, he said simply, "On target. Keep it coming."

ON THE GROUND, neither Fetterman nor Gerber had heard the chopper, but assumed one must be around somewhere. They saw the VC attack destroyed before it got launched. The first round had landed among the assembling enemy soldiers, and the barrage landed in the trees where they had been massing. They had fired into the sky, but it did them no good.

"Christ, look at that," said Fetterman. "Right on target. Fucking beautiful."

For a moment, Gerber watched as the artillery ripped apart the assault force. He wanted to cheer, even as he realized that men were dying, but he didn't. Instead, he said, "You take charge here. I'm going to check on the rest of the hamlet."

He dropped away from the perimeter and ran across the hamlet. On the way he encountered the body of a dead striker and took the weapon from it. He continued until he got to the dispensary.

"How are things here?"

Washington was crouched over the body of a man, his hands covered in blood. Morrow was kneeling at the wounded man's head, holding on to him.

"We need help," said Washington. "We don't get some of these people out of here, they're going to die. How are things outside?"

"Outside it couldn't be better. We've a guardian angel somewhere, calling in artillery."

"Can we get a chopper in here?" asked Washington.

"We'll do what we can." Gerber raced out again, running for the hootch where the Navy man was working on the radios. He found him, sitting in the middle of a pile of parts but with nothing that worked.

"How long?"

"I don't know. I don't think I'll ever be able to get enough working pieces for a single set. They sure chopped them up good. They did their job."

"Keep at it," said Gerber, "but I think we'll have a chopper in here soon."

The man dropped the part he held and shrugged. "Then why keep at it?"

"Just in case the chopper doesn't make it. T.J. said we've got people we need to evacuate."

"I'll do my best."

But even as he spoke, they heard the helicopter approaching from the south. Gerber looked up. A dark shape raced across the rice paddies, low, using the hamlet to shield itself from the enemy in the tree line on the opposite side of the hamlet, and from the artillery that was still falling.

At first it was nothing more than a noise in the distance and then a black shape coming at him. Then he could see it easily as it passed over the berm. It hovered there for a moment, the rotor wash picking up the debris and dirt and swirling it into a whirlwind. The landing light stabbed out, then was gone. The chopper settled to the ground.

For a moment, Gerber stood and stared. As two men got out of the cargo compartment, he knew it was over. They again had communication with the outside world. If the enemy had any more surprises for them, they could be countered easily. All the support the Americans had to offer was again available.

Gerber trotted toward the chopper to welcome his guests to the former hamlet of Duc Bang. It wouldn't be much of a welcome because there wasn't much left of the hamlet, but at least the battle was over. It was too late now for the enemy to do anything but get out.

16

THE HAMLET OF DUC BANG

The cleared area to the south of the hamlet began to look like the parking area for the fly-in guests of an air show. Half a dozen choppers sat on the ground, their blades tied down. Another half dozen circled overhead, where TV film crews were trying to get good visuals for the evening news. Only two reporters, other than Robin Morrow, had bothered to land and both of them worked for newspapers.

Gerber stood at the edge of the berm and watched the assembly of congressmen, brass hats, aides, secretaries and newspapermen walk the field outside the camp. They stayed away from the foul-smelling water of the rice paddies where there was more floating on the surface than just the bodies of the men killed the night before.

One congressman put a foot on the back of a dead VC, stuck a hand in his khaki safari jacket and pushed his hat back on his head. It was a parody of the big-game hunter pictures that came out of Africa at the turn of the century. A young woman in a short skirt and a see-through blouse snapped a picture of the hero.

"So what's happening now?"

Gerber turned and saw Morrow, still wearing her sweat and bloodstained jumpsuit. Her hair was a mess and her face dirty.

"The congressmen are assessing the value of the strategic hamlet concept by studying the dead around here. One of them found an AK we missed during the morning sweep. He's given it to an aide to guard for him."

Morrow put a hand to her eyes and looked up at the choppers circling like vultures waiting for something to die. "That the guards for the congressmen?"

"Strangely enough, it's not. Those are members of the fourth estate, getting the whole story for the nightly news."

Morrow shrugged but offered no alibis for the press. Instead she took out her camera and photographed the scene in front of her: fifteen or twenty bodies lying on the area cleared by the bulldozer, mangled men who had been bled white by their wounds. The ground where they lay and their clothing were stained a strange shade of rusty brown. Around them were the men and women flown out from Saigon to examine the field.

"If there's a smartass VC sniper in the trees, he could get himself a couple of congressmen and a few generals, if he wants. I tried to warn them, but everyone assumes it's safe now."

"Make a good story," said Morrow.

Gerber laughed. "And it would probably end my career."

"Nah," she said. "I'd write it up so that you'd be the hero. You'd have to return to the World for a medal and start a tour. Write a book and go to Hollywood to star in a movie."

"Be better than sweating to death out here."

Padgett broke off from the group and headed over to Gerber. Before he was close, Morrow said, "I'll buy you dinner in Saigon when you get back."

"Don't you want to talk to the general?"

"No thanks. I've talked to enough of them today."

She left as Padgett arrived. "Sorry," he said. "I didn't mean to chase away your girlfriend."

"She's a reporter, not my girlfriend," said Gerber, not sure that the general believed him.

Padgett stood there, hands on his hips and pipe stuck in his mouth. He nodded. "Strategic hamlets proved their worth here. Damn, we got what, two hundred, two hundred and fifty?"

"There are seventy-two bodies on the field. Artillery got most of them."

"Whatever. What are our casualties like?"

"Pretty heavy, I'm afraid. Thirty-four strikers dead, five Americans killed and a number of them wounded. All have been evaced. Seabees took their bulldozer and got out this morning. Infantry followed them. Only Americans left are my Special Forces troops. Couple of us took some shrapnel, but no one was hurt bad."

"You get a list of the names and I'll see that they get their Purple Hearts."

"That's been taken care of."

"Good. Now I think the congressman will believe me when I tell him that the strategic hamlets are the way to end our involvement in the war."

"How so?" asked Gerber, surprised.

"Look around you, man. Sure, we've got to rebuild, but here's a hamlet the VC couldn't overrun. Proves the value of the concept."

"General," said Gerber, "the strategic hamlet concept had nothing to do with this. There happened to be three, four hundred men here to protect the hamlet and we didn't make it. Not one structure is standing intact. Not one. Most are little more than a pile of burned rubble, but even that's not the important fact."

"And what is that, Captain?"

"There are no Vietnamese farmers here. They all got out yesterday. We defended the area with our guns and artillery, and the Vietnamese had nothing to do with it."

"I warn you, Captain, don't say a word about that to the congressmen."

"And if they ask where the farmers are?"

"Tell them the locals were evaced this morning. They were given medical treatment, breakfast, and they'll be returning just as soon as we can get some shelter provided for them."

Gerber turned and stared at the general. "You're going to go on with this myth about the strategic hamlet?"

"It's policy, Captain. I'd suggest you endorse it if you want to remain a captain and not become a sergeant."

"Yes, sir," said Gerber.

"Now, I'm going off to see that the congressmen get the right idea about this place. I'll count on you to back me up on it."

"Yes, sir."

As the general walked off, Morrow returned. "You get your instructions."

"Yeah, I got them. That offer of dinner include a drink?"

"As big as you want."

"Then you're on."

She grinned and said, "See you in Saigon."

GLOSSARY

AC—Aircraft commander. The pilot in charge of an aircraft.

ADO—An A-Detachment's area of operations.

AFVN—Armed forces radio and television network in Vietnam. Army PFC Pat Sajak is probably the most memorable of AFVN's DJs with his loud and long, "GOOOOOOOOOOOOD MORNing, Vietnam!" The spinning Wheel of Fortune gives no clues to his whereabouts today.

AK-47—Assault rifle usually used by the North Vietnamese and the Vietcong.

AO—Area of operations.

AO DAI—Long dresslike garment, slit up the sides and worn over pants.

AP ROUNDS—Armor-piercing ammunition.

APU—Auxiliary power unit. An outside source of power used to start aircraft engines.

ARC LIGHT—Term used for a B-52 bombing mission. Also known as heavy arty.

ARVN—Army of the Republic of Vietnam. A South Vietnamese soldier. Also known as Marvin Arvin.

ASA—Army Security Agency.

AST—Control officer between men in isolation and the outside world, responsible for taking care of all problems.

AUTOVON—Army phone system that allows soldiers on base to call another base, bypassing the civilian phone system.

BISCUIT—Term that refers to C-rations.

BODY COUNT—Number of enemy killed, wounded or captured during an operation. Term used by Saigon and Washington to measure progress of the war.

BOOM BOOM—A term used by Vietnamese prostitutes in selling their product.

BOONDOGGLE—Any military operation that hasn't been completely thought out. An operation that is ridiculous.

BOONIE HATS—Soft caps worn by the grunts in the field when they were not wearing their steel pots.

BUSHMASTER—Jungle warfare expert or soldier skilled in jungle navigation. Also a large deadly snake not common to Vietnam but mighty tasty.

BX—Base Exchange. A sort of military department store. Also PX for Post Exchange.

C AND C—Command and Control aircraft that circles overhead to direct combined air and ground operations.

CABLES—Army slang for loose threads on the uniform.

CAO BOIS—Cowboys, criminals of Saigon who rode motorcycles.

CARIBOU—Cargo transport plane.

CHINOOK—Army Aviation twin-engine helicopter. A CH-47. Also known as a shit hook.

CHOCK—Term that refers to the number of aircraft in a flight. Chock Three is the third, Chock Six is the sixth.

CLAYMORE—Antipersonnel mine that fires 750 steel balls with a lethal range of 50 meters.

CLOSE AIR SUPPORT—Use of airplanes and helicopters to fire on enemy units near friendlies.

CO CONG—Female Vietcong.

CONEX—Steel container about ten feet height, ten feet deep and ten feet long used to haul equipment and supplies.

DAI UY—Vietnamese army rank, equivalent of Captain.

DEROS—Date of estimated return from overseas.

DIRNSA—Director, National Security Agency.

E AND E—Escape and Evasion.

FEET WET—Term used by pilots to describe flight over water.

FIVE—Radio call sign for the executive officer of a unit.

FOB—Forward operating base.

FOX MIKE—FM radio.

FNG—Fucking new guy.

FREEDOM BIRD—Name given to any aircraft that takes troops out of Vietnam. Usually refers to the commercial jet flights that took men back to the World.

GARAND—The M-1 rifle that was replaced by the M-14. Issued to the Vietnamese early in the war.

GO TO HELL RAG—Towel or any large cloth worn around the neck by grunts.

GRAIL—NATO name for the shoulder-fired SA-7 surface-to-air missile.

GUARD THE RADIO—Stand by in the commo bunker and listen for messages.

GUIDELINE—NATO name for SA-2 surface-to-air missiles.

GUNSHIP—Armed helicopter or cargo plane that carries weapons instead of cargo.

GUN TARGET LINE—Path an artillery shell follows from the gun to the target.

HALO—High Altitude Low Opening. A type of parachute jump.

HE—High-explosive ammunition.

HOOTCH—Almost any shelter, from temporary to long-term.

HORN—Specific kind of radio operations that uses satellites to rebroadcast messages.

HORSE—See Biscuit.

HOTEL THREE—Helicopter landing area at Saigon's Tan Son Nhut Airport.

HUEY—UH-1 helicopter.

IN-COUNTRY—Term used to refer to American troops operating in South Vietnam.

INTELLIGENCE—Any information about enemy operations that would be useful in planning a mission. It can include troop movements, weapons capabilities, biographies of enemy commanders and general information about terrain features.

KABAR—Type of military combat knife.

KIA—Killed in action. (Since the United States was not engaged in a declared war, the use of the term KIA was not authorized. KIA came to mean enemy dead. Americans were KHA, killed in hostile action.)

KLICK—One thousand meters. A kilometer.

LIMA LIMA—Land line. Refers to telephone communications between two points on the ground.

LLDB—Luc Luong Dac Biet. South Vietnamese Special Forces. Sometimes referred to as the Look Long, Duck Back.

LP—Listening Post. A position outside the perimeter manned by a couple of soldiers to give advance warning of enemy activity.

LSA—Lubricant used by soldiers on their weapons to ensure that they will continue to operate properly.

·LZ—Landing zone.

M-3A1—A .45 caliber submachine gun that was favored by GIs in World War II because its slow rate of fire meant the barrel didn't rise and they didn't burn through their ammo as fast as they did with some other weapons. Also known as a grease gun.

M-14—Standard rifle of the United States forces, eventually replaced by the M-16. It fires the standard NATO round—7.62 mm.

M-16—Standard infantry weapon of the Vietnam War. It fires 5.56 mm ammunition.

M-79—Short-barreled, shoulder-fired weapon that fires a 40 mm grenade. These can be high explosives, white phosphorus or canister.

MACV—Military Assistance Command, Vietnam, replaced MAAG in 1964.

MEDEVAC—Helicopter used to take the wounded to medical facilities. Also called dustoff.

MIA—Missing in action.

MONOPOLY MONEY—Term used by servicemen in Vietnam to describe the MPC handed out in lieu of regular United States currency.

MOS—Military Occupation Specialty. It is a job description.

MPC—Military Payment Certificates. The monopoly money used instead of real cash.

NCO—Noncommissioned officer. A noncom. A sergeant.

NCOIC—NCO in charge. The senior NCO in a unit, detachment or patrol.

NDB—Nondirectional beacon. A radio beacon that can be used for homing.

NEXT—The next man to be rotated home. See Short-timer.

NINETEEN—Average age of the combat soldier in Vietnam, as opposed to twenty-six in World War II.

NOUC-MAM—Foul-smelling fish sauce used by the Vietnamese.

NVA—North Vietnamese army. Also used to designate a soldier from North Vietnam.

OD—Olive drab.

P (PIASTER)—Basic monetary unit in South Vietnam, worth slightly less than a penny.

PETA-PRIME—Black, tarlike substance that melts in the heat of the day to become a sticky, black nightmare that clings to boots, clothes and equipment. It was used to hold down the dust during the dry season.

PETER PILOT—Copilot in a helicopter.

PLF—Parachute Landing Fall. The roll used by parachutists on landing.

POW—Prisoner of war.

PRC-10—Portable radio.

PRC-25—Lighter portable radio that replaced the PRC-10.

PULL PITCH—Term used by helicopter pilots that means they are going to take off.

PUNGI STAKE—Sharpened bamboo hidden to penetrate the foot, sometimes dipped in feces.

PUZZLE PALACE—The Pentagon. It was called the puzzle palace because no one knew what was going on there. Puzzle Palace East referred to MACV or USARV Headquarters in Saigon.

RINGKNOCKER—Graduate of a military academy. The term refers to the ring worn by all graduates.

RON—Remain overnight. A term used by flight crews to indicate a flight that will last longer than a day.

RPD—Soviet-made 7.62 mm light machine gun.

RTO—Radio Telephone Operator. The radioman of a unit.

RUFF-PUFFS—Term applied to the RF-PFs, the regional forces and popular forces. Militia drawn from the local population.

SA-2—Surface-to-air missile fired from a fixed site. It is a radar-guided missile nearly 35 feet long. Also called Guideline.

SA-7—Surface-to-air missile that is shoulder-fired and infrared homing. Also called Grail.

SACSA—Special Assistant for Counterinsurgency and Special Activities.

SAFE AREA—Selected area for evasion. It doesn't mean the area is safe from the enemy, only that the terrain, location or local population make the area a good place for escape and evasion.

SAM TWO—Refers to the SA-2 Guideline missile.

SAR—Search and rescue. SAR forces are the people involved in search-and-rescue missions.

SHIT HOOK—See Chinook.

SHORT-TIME—GI term for a quickie.

SHORT-TIMER—Person who had been in Vietnam for nearly a year and who would be rotated back to the World soon. When the DEROS (Date of estimated return from overseas) was the shortest in the unit, the person was said to be ''next.''

SINGLE DIGIT MIDGET—Soldier with fewer than ten days left in-country.

SIX—Radio call sign for the unit commander.

SKS—Soviet-made carbine.

SMG—Submachine gun.

SOI—Signal operating instructions. The booklet that contained the call signs and radio frequencies of the units in Vietnam.

SOP—Standard operating procedure.

SPIKE TEAM—Special Forces team made up for a direct action mission.

STEEL POT—Standard United States Army helmet. The steel pot was the outer, metal cover.

TEAM UNIFORM OR COMPANY UNIFORM—UHF radio frequency on which the team or the company communicates. Frequencies are changed periodically in an attempt to confuse the enemy.

THE WORLD—United States.

THREE—Radio call sign of the operations officer.

THREE CORPS—Military area around Saigon. Vietnam was divided into four corps areas.

TO & E—Table of Organization and Equipment. A detailed listing of all the men and equipment assigned to a unit.

TOC—Tactical operations center.

TOT—Time over target. The time at which aircraft are supposed to be over a drop zone with parachutists, or over a target if the planes are bombers.

TRICK CHIEF—NCOIC for a shift.

TRIPLE A—Antiaircraft artillery or AAA. Anything used to shoot at airplanes or helicopters.

TWO—Radio call sign of the intelligence officer.

TWO-OH-ONE (201) FILE—Military records file that lists all a soldier's qualifications, training, experience and abilities. It is passed from unit to unit so that a new commander will have some idea about the capabilities of an incoming soldier.

UMZ—Ultramilitarized zone, the name GIs gave to the DMZ (Demilitarized Zone).

UNIFORM—Refers to the UHF radio. Company uniform is the frequency assigned to a company.

USARV—United States Army, Vietnam.

VC—Vietcong, called Victor Charlie (phonetic alphabet), or just Charlie.

VIETCONG—Contraction of Vietnam Cong San (Vietnamese Communist).

VIETCONG SAN—Vietnamese Communists. A term in use since 1956.

WHITE MICE—Term that referred to the Vietnamese military police, because they wore white helmets.

WIA—Wounded in action.

WILLIE PETE—WP, white phosphorus, called smoke rounds. Also used as antipersonnel weapons.

WSO—Weapons System Officer. The man who rides in the back seat of a Phantom, because he is responsible for the weapons systems.

XO—Executive officer of a unit.

ZAP—To ding, pop caps or shoot. To kill.

**Adventure and suspense
in a treacherous new world**

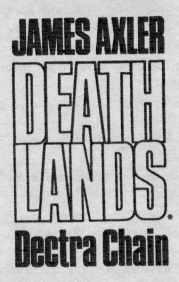

JAMES AXLER
DEATH
LANDS.
Dectra Chain

Ryan Cawdor and his band of postholocaust survivors become
caught up in a horrifying nightmare after they materialize in a
nineteenth-century Maine whaling village and Ryan is shang-
haied by a ferocious captain, who will go to any length to man
her whaling ship.

Available now at your favorite retail outlet, or reserve your copy for shipping by sending your
name, address, zip or postal code along with a check or money order for $4.70 (includes
75¢ for postage and handling) payable to Gold Eagle Books;

In the U.S.	In Canada
Gold Eagle Books	Gold Eagle Books
901 Fuhrmann Blvd.	P.O. Box 609
Box 1325	Fort Erie, Ontario
Buffalo, NY 14269-1325	L2A 5X3

Please specify book title with your order.

DL-7A

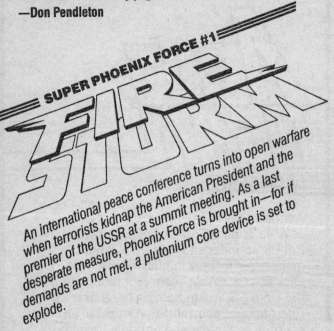

Mack Bolan's

by Dick Stivers

Action writhes in the reader's own streets
as Able Team's Carl "Ironman" Lyons,
Pol Blancanales and Gadgets Schwarz
make triple trouble in blazing war. Join
Dick Stivers's Able Team as it returns to
the United States to become the country's
finest tactical neutralization squad in an
era of urban terror and unbridled crime.

"Able Team will go anywhere, do anything,
in order to complete their mission. Plenty
of action! Recommended!"
—*West Coast Review of Books*

Able Team titles are available
wherever paperbacks are sold.

AT-1

TAKE 'EM NOW

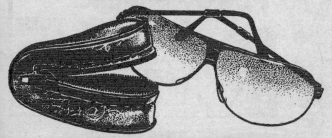

FOLDING SUNGLASSES
FROM GOLD EAGLE

Mean up your act with these tough, street-smart shades. Practical, too, because they fold 3 times into a handy, zip-up polyurethane pouch that fits neatly into your pocket. Rugged metal frame. Scratch-resistant acrylic lenses. Best of all, they can be yours for only $6.99.

MAIL YOUR ORDER TODAY.

Send your name, address, and zip code, along with a check or money order for just $6.99 + .75¢ for postage and handling (for a total of $7.74) payable to Gold Eagle Reader Service. (New York and Iowa residents please add applicable sales tax.)

Remove from pouch...

unfold once...

unfold twice...

and they're ready to wear.

Gold Eagle Reader Service
901 Fuhrmann Blvd.
P.O. Box 1396
Buffalo, N.Y. 14240-1396

GES-1A

Offer not available in Canada.